BRUTAL BOND

SAVAGELY DEPRAVED

J.L. QUICK

COVER DESIGN: Morally Gray Publishing
EDITING: Spice Me Up Editing (Katie)
PROOFREADING: Spice Me Up Editing (Kendra)

To the dirty little pain sluts that like when it stings so good...

This one might hurt.

AUTHOR'S NOTE

This novel is a contemporary dark romance. It contains scenes and descriptive adult content, recommended for adult (18+) readers.

As a contemporary dark romance, this novel is not intended to be a portrayal of a healthy relationship or a 'how to guide' for the kink and lifestyle elements depicted within.

For those interested in exploring aspects of the kink and/or dominant-submissive relationships explored in the following chapters, please do so responsibly and with appropriate reference materials.

TRIGGER WARNINGS

This novel is a contemporary dark romance. It contains scenes and descriptive adult content that might be triggering for some readers.

Please review the content warnings at the link below.

THE DEVILS OF ADELAIDE COVE

"One pain is lessened by another's anguish."

—— **William Shakespeare, Romeo & Juliet**

BEFORE YOU GET STARTED...

Brutal Bond is the continuation of the Savagely Depraved series. To fully understand the events that are going to unfold in these pages, I highly recommend starting with Dark Devils (the prequel novella to the Savagely Depraved series), and reading this series in chronological order.

The entire series is available for purchase on Amazon.

CHAPTER ONE

EDMUND

"It took a while to get you all on board, but I'm glad we've managed to come to an agreement." I shake hands with the white-haired men sitting across from me as we finish up our meeting.

Walking from the building, I reach for the phone that has been buzzing incessantly in my jacket pocket for the past ten minutes. As I swipe it open, I'm met with a barrage of missed calls and nearly twice as many text messages.

My heart pounds as I quickly read them. Fear, rage, and helplessness course through me when two more pop up on the screen.

He's here.

He won't stop banging on the door.

As though my body is acting without thought, I race toward my car. Trying to run at full speed, yet feeling like my feet are encased in cement as the car appears to be slowly seeping further away in the distance.

I need to fucking get to her.

My chest heaves as I push myself harder, my heart thumping painfully hard in my chest when I reach my car. The moment I open the door, I quickly slide onto the hot, sunbaked leather of the driver's seat. I barely have the door pulled shut when I push the button to start the engine and stomp on the accelerator, my tires squealing against the pavement.

Hurtling from my parking space, I push the button on the dash. I can't get her details up fast enough to call her back. It barely rings before she picks up, her fast and ragged breaths blasting through my speakers.

She's fucking terrified, shakily breathing my name, "Eddie..."

"Fuck," I hiss, gripping the steering wheel to the point that my knuckles begin to whiten. Trying to remain calm for her, I soothingly tell her, "I'm on my way."

Without a second thought, I ignore the posted speed limits and swerve around cars as I drive through town at reckless speeds to get to the highway. Veering around a white sedan stopped in the intersection, I make a hard right-hand turn, my tires screeching their complaint along the asphalt.

The fists hammering on her door are so loud that they pound through the subwoofer in my trunk.

Thump. Thump. THUMP!

BRUTAL BOND   3

"Eddie," her voice trembles, "he's going to break through the door."

Thump. Thump. THUMP!

"I'm coming." I round the onramp to the interstate hastily, only to floor it the second I merge into traffic. "I'm coming for you. I promise."

This drive usually takes me about twenty-five minutes, and right now, that's way too fucking long. Glancing down at the dash as I weave between the other cars, the speedometer reads 141 miles per hour.

Not fast enough.

The wood door cracking echoes through the confines of my car, only to be drowned out by her cries.

"Get in Nikki's bedroom," I yell, "It'll buy you a little time. And lock the fucking door."

"Ed—"

"Just fucking do it," I shout over her.

The only response I get is her shrill shrieks muffling the splintering of the wood door.

He's inside.

Screams fill the car; gut-wrenching cries that tear at my heart. Her screams fall quiet and are followed by loud crashes and shattering glass. The phone clatters against the floor, and suddenly, everything sounds so far away. Yet, there is no denying the hell occurring on the other end.

"Please…" she sobs in between groans and more items crashing to the ground. "No…."

Stomping on the clutch and shifting, I press the accelerator further to the floor. The speedometer quickly climbs to 163 miles per hour.

A deep, gruff voice comes through the speakers. "What's the matter? I thought you liked it fucking rough."

My blood boils, and heat floods up my neck and over my face. Every bit of me shakes—not with fear, but pure unadulterated rage—and I violently squeeze the steering wheel as I yell into the Bluetooth, "You're a fucking dead man."

Five more miles.

Every strike I listen to her endure causes me to flinch. Hit after hit, her screams and grunts slowly diminish until there's nothing but silence.

Absolutely terrifying silence.

CHAPTER TWO

EDMUND

About Two Months Ago

Sitting at my desk, I aimlessly scroll through women on a fetish dating app.

What a last desperate fucking resort!

Blonde—pretty, obnoxiously fake tits.

Swipe.

Brunette—fucking stunning, seeking a Daddy.

Swipe.

Brunette—perfect tits, domme.

Ha!

Swipe.

I've found a few that are pretty—absolutely gorgeous even but not one that is into my brand of kink.

While the women Liz procures for me are always willing—
or at least subservient enough to take what I give—these
women don't seem like they would fit that same bill.

I'm about to close the app when a text from Grant pops up
on the screen.

> **GRANT**
> Detective Asshole is on the hunt again.

Fuck, he's determined to ruin everything.

And ensure we're all in prison for the rest of our lives.

> Party is on.

I need to fuck someone.

To mark someone.

To watch them enjoy my pain.

> I got rid of Chloe a few weeks ago, and if I
> don't stick my dick in something soon....

Chloe was fun for a few months. Liz always does a good job
of finding girls for all of us—an exceptionally hard chal-
lenge with our varied interests. But like any girl that had
come before, I tired of her. Her appeal dwindled quickly
when she lost her enthusiasm for my brand of play. She
only stayed around as long as she did because she was a
good fuck.

*Even if she didn't love my pain the same way she did the night
we met.*

I probably should've just sent her on her way when I first grew bored with her. Letting her stay gave her the opportunity to learn a bit too much about me and my friends, leaving only one option.

And it wasn't a hefty check and an NDA.

Being swamped at work since her disposal hasn't left me time to find another suitable plaything. My new assistant, Aubrey, has been at the top of my list for the past two weeks. Between her long, blonde hair and the Marilyn Monroe curves she carries, I can hardly peel my eyes away from her.

Unfortunately, she is an absolute tease—*a relentless fucking flirt*—with a body built for sin and a moral compass that seems to prevent her from getting fucked by her boss.

I need to fuck something.

Something that isn't my fucking hand.

And I must be horny as hell if I'm even thinking about fucking Will to get to Liz.

> Let's just say I may be liable to finally take Liz up on her offer.

> **WILL**
> Keep the party on, I don't want his dick anywhere near me.

A few more texts are shared between us, confirming that we will not be canceling tomorrow night's festivities.

Thank fucking God.

CHAPTER THREE

HARPER

"Can I borrow your mascara," Nikki shouts as she lets herself into my bathroom.

"This isn't the worst idea we've ever had, is it?" I respond over the spray of the shower. When she doesn't answer, I pull back the shower curtain to ensure she didn't grab my mascara and run. I find her standing at the bathroom sink, curling her hair. "Nik?"

"I was working out how to answer." She unwinds the curling iron from her long, blonde hair before turning to face me. "You fucked Cal, right?"

"Football Cal?" I clarify.

"Yes," she rolls her eyes. "Did you fuck another Cal too?"

"No," I laugh. "And yes, I fucked Football Cal."

"And what did you get for that?"

"You mean other than a Plan B?" I jest.

"Exactly." She flails her hands in the air and returns to curling her hair. "You date all these college boys, and you're lucky to get a cheeseburger and a beer out of them. Even luckier if they even remotely try and make you come."

She's not wrong.

The last guy I went out with was under the impression that three items off the dollar menu had basically paid for his right to fuck me in the ass. Considering how absolutely oblivious he was to the concept of foreplay—*or a clitoris*—my ass was definitely not on the menu for him.

"This is one night," she continues. "We suck it up and let some rich, fat, old bald dude that probably can't even keep it up without a little blue pill fuck us for the night. Then, we come home with enough money to pay off our undergrad student loans. And still have enough left over to pay for grad school, our apartment, a new car, and a shit ton of fun for a while."

"It's an investment," I summarize.

"Exactly!" she exclaims. "Do you know of an easier way to make a million dollars? I don't make near that with any of the Daddies I date."

I shake my head and mutter, "I guess I'm just nervous."

Unlike Nikki, I haven't taken the sugar daddy plunge yet. I signed up for the app with her a few months ago—which I'm sure is how they found me for tonight's party—but I haven't actually gone on a date or met up with any of the guys on there. Letting some disgusting old guy sweat all over me for a few minutes doesn't quite seem worth it.

Although the apartment Nikki's current Daddy is basically footing the bill for is quite nice.

Way nicer than either of us could afford.

"It's just sex," she shrugs. "What is there to be nervous about? It's not like you're selling your virginity. You've fucked plenty of guys for the hell of it. I know, I've been there for several of them."

"Twice," I correct her. Not that it makes a difference. "We've fucked two guys together. And I've told you, it's not the same for me as it is for you."

"And I'm telling you, I still don't believe you. No one eats pussy like that and doesn't actually enjoy it," she smirks.

"Whatever." I throw a hand towel at her as she walks from the bathroom.

It's not a lie.

She's the only woman I've ever been with—always as the two of us joining a guy—but I'm definitely not sexually attracted to her or any other woman for that matter. They just don't do it for me. I do enjoy it, though. I come. She comes. It's fun, but that's it.

Sex with men isn't much different, other than the coming part most of the time. *That usually doesn't happen.* There is no denying that I like men, but something about sex is missing. It's definitely not the fireworks and explosions that I hear some girls talk about.

The closest I get to that is the drawer of power tools in my nightstand.

"Ten minutes," Nik pops her head back in the doorway. "The driver just texted, and he'll be here in ten minutes."

"Fuck." I hastily apply the last of my makeup.

"Don't worry. I already laid the clothes they sent over on your bed." She sets my mascara on the vanity. "And I'm just going to go on record here, I could get very used to five-hundred-dollar panties."

"To what?" I scoff.

"Did you not look in your box earlier? La Perla lingerie, Valentino dresses, and Jimmy Choos." She slides her hands over the sleek black dress hugging her body. "You don't go back to off-the-rack stuff after this."

Quickly finishing my makeup, I head to my room and look at the clothes spread across the foot of my bed. They are gorgeous. Luxurious. And they probably cost as much as a month's rent for our apartment.

It's one night.

How bad could it be?

CHAPTER
FOUR

EDMUND

Sitting at the bar while we wait for Grant and his newest pet to arrive for tonight's festivities, I sip my gin and tonic and aimlessly scroll through my phone until I wind up reading emails for work.

Is this what my life has come to?

At a fucking party, waiting to dip my cock in a gorgeous and over-eager co-ed, and I'm reading my fucking work email.

The barstool beside me scratches across the hardwood floor as it's pulled from the bar, and I look up from my phone to find Samuel taking a seat beside me. As much as he grates on my last nerve with his impulsivity, he is a welcome distraction to the deep dive I was about to take into my own psyche.

We talk for a bit, waiting for Grant to arrive with his new plaything. I'm more than eager to see if she is as beautiful in person as she was in the photo he sent of her, even if the chance of getting to play with her is going to be slim.

Apparently, I'm too rough with everyone's toys.

"No one is saying you can't enjoy yourself. Or have a little fun." I stand from my stool and give Samuel's shoulder a brotherly squeeze when Grant arrives. He's a pain in the ass, but I do actually like the kid. "Just clean up after yourself."

"No loose ends." He nods as I cross the room toward the gorgeous blonde on Grant's arm. She is every bit as stunning as her photo. More so. She's petite, with a thin yet athletic build and subtle curves. Her long blonde hair is curled and pulled over her shoulder, exposing her back.

A gorgeous back of pristine porcelain skin.

Fuck, she would mark so well for me.

"You're fucking gorgeous." I step closer to her and run my hand down her bare spine. She jumps at my touch, causing my cock to twitch with excitement. Letting my fingers linger on her soft skin, I turn my attention to Grant. "Please tell me every inch of her skin is this fucking glorious."

"It is." He cocks a brow. "But there is no way in hell you're going to leave a single mark on it."

Well, fuck. He sure knows how to ruin a party.

At least my *party.*

Rounding the room and heading back to the bar, I grab my drink while Liz and Will firmly secure their place between the thighs of Grant's stunning pet.

Fuck, I'd pay just to have the opportunity to watch Liz fuck her.

"Two million," Liz pants as she pulls back from Will. "Eddie, love, you get Will's and Grant's too."

Oh! Fuck yes!

Apparently, I have no need to fantasize about Liz fucking Grant's pet. I'm going to get to watch several women feast on each other as I fuck them all. My cock throbs at the mere thought of all the pussy and ass waiting down the hall.

"What the fuck, he gets both of them?" Samuel huffs.

"Maybe when you learn to behave outside of this house, we'll treat you a little better, kid," I quip. My comment is made in jest, but based on the look spreading across Samuel's face, it may not have been received as such.

That'll be a matter for another time.

Given the choice between apologizing to him and having pussy, he's not getting my attention right now.

Downing the last of my gin and tonic, I slam it onto the bar before heading out of the lounge. I make my way down the hall toward the room where we segregate the women until we're ready for them. While a little socializing would be more fun, this way tends to emphasize the fact that tonight is purely transactional. They give us their bodies, and we give them money. Small talk—and even names—are totally optional.

Eager to see what Liz has procured for us this evening, my steps are light and quick along the long hallway to the other wing of the house.

Hopefully, not another woman with abhorrent fake tits.

Blondes?

Brunettes?

After opening the door, I cross the threshold and step into the room, momentarily stopping in my tracks.

A fucking redhead.

There are four undeniably beautiful women waiting in the room. All of them dressed impeccably in well-fitted designer lingerie and heels. Each of them absolutely stunning, yet I can barely pull my eyes from the fiery redhead. Brushing her hair behind her ear, she tips her face up to me, and I'm met with her sparkling blue eyes.

They're deep. Telling. She's nervous but excited. Her eyes are full of intrigue.

She wants to know what this world is all about.

And fuck do I ever plan on showing her.

"You. You are definitely mine tonight." I curl my finger in her direction. I'm so fucking enthralled with her that I couldn't care less about the fact that Liz granted me three women tonight. "Pick the two you want to join us."

CHAPTER
FIVE

HARPER

As footsteps come down the hall, my eyes fall to my lap as I try to catch my breath and slow my racing heart. Nikki grabs my hand and gives it a light squeeze before she whispers, "If you're having doubts, you don't have to do this."

I don't have a chance to respond before I hear the footsteps come to a stop in the doorway. I take a deep breath in and exhale it slowly.

You can do this.

Brushing my hair from my face and tucking it behind my ear, I look up to find the source of the footsteps.

Fuck.

He isn't even close to an old, fat, bald dude.

More like the polar opposite. He can't be older than my dad.

Gross, Harper.

Let's not think about that again tonight.

He's tall and fit, with a thick head of dark brown hair. The well-trimmed beard perfectly frames his angled jawline. But it's his eyes I'm locked on. They're not quite blue, but more of a deep, slate gray. I've never seen anything like them before.

He stares back at me, and his gaze bores straight through me. I want to divert my eyes, but I can't seem to look away from him.

"You." His voice is deep and broody. "You are definitely mine tonight."

He points at me and curls his finger in a come-hither motion, and I swallow hard. I don't know what I was expecting tonight, but this wasn't it. I'm about to stand from the couch when he commands, "Pick the two you want to join us."

The what?

I squeeze Nikki's hand. She talked me into coming, and I'll be damned if she's going to abandon me now. I muster the courage to speak and gesture to Nikki and the blonde girl sitting across from me. "These two."

"Edmund." He extends his hand to help me from the couch. I accept it, and his touch tingles across my palm.

"Harper." I stare up at him as I stand inches from him.

Fuck, he even smells good.

"Ladies." He gestures toward the door. Not entirely sure where I'm heading, I lead the way with the three of them following behind me. I nearly bump into a massive—*also totally hot and not old*—man.

"Sorry, kid," Edmund smirks as he slips his arms around Nikki and the blonde. "I'm not a selfish prick. Grab your girl and come join us."

Come what?

Relief washes over me when the big guy passes. I wasn't expecting to have a foursome tonight, an orgy might've pushed me over my breaking point.

"The door on the right," Edmund's rich voice billows from behind me. Reaching the double wooden doors, I turn the handle and push it open. Every sex toy imaginable hangs from the wall. So many that I don't even know what some of them are called.

Edmund walks straight to a cabinet and begins pulling out sets of leather cuffs—*handcuffs*. He binds Nikki's hands and then the blonde's without speaking a word.

"Tell me, ladies. Do you like it to hurt a little?" He's speaking to all of us, but he stares into my eyes through every word as though he's only talking to me. Dragging his fingers lightly down my forearms, he slips the cuffs around my wrists and secures the buckles. Hooking them together, he doesn't let go. Instead, he holds my bound wrists in his large hands and continues to gaze into my eyes. "Because it's going to hurt."

Swallowing hard, I suddenly feel like my heart is trying to burst free from the confines of my ribcage. My breathing immediately accelerates to the same rapid pace. His eyes dip to my heaving chest for a moment, and a devilish smirk ticks at the corner of his mouth.

Fuck, that's hot.

Using the short chain between the two cuffs, he leads me across the room to a wall lined with dark-stained wooden beams. Reaching the wall, he drops the cuffs and turns my back to him. He steps close—*so fucking close his chest presses against me*—and places his hands on my shoulders.

He takes his time sliding them down my arms, and my skin burns like it is on fire from his touch alone. His heavy breaths blow against my neck as he reaches my wrists and lifts them above my head. Securing them over a hook, his fingers trail back down my arms, and I can't stifle the whimper that trembles over my lips.

"I can feel how excited you are, Harper." His hands continue to slide down my body and around my waist. Breathing hard, his lips dust against the back of my ear, and he whispers, "Is it fear or intrigue?"

"Both," I answer breathlessly.

I'm fucking terrified.

It was curiosity that killed the cat, wasn't it?

I just never realized that meant my pussy.

CHAPTER
SIX

HARPER

"Hmmmm." He growls against my neck as he pulls from me, and his grumble travels straight to my core. His fingers trail down my thighs as he kneels behind me, and he groans, "All this perfect alabaster skin. You're going to be so fucking beautiful all marked for me."

Marked?

His teeth sink in the flesh of my ass cheek. The unexpected bite is hard, and the sudden stabbing pain causes me to yelp. It hurts like fucking hell, but my inability to breathe has nothing to do with the searing pain. Loosening the hold with his teeth, he sucks gently as he lets go and places a soft kiss over the tooth marks he left behind.

"I'm going to fucking enjoy you." His voice is dark as he stands behind me. He places a firm smack on my other cheek before turning his attention to Nikki and the blonde, both of whom I had forgotten were even in the room.

My arms bound above my head and forehead nearly resting on the wall, I can barely see what's happening behind me. Watching from the corner of my eye, Edmund leads the two of them to the wall beside me.

"Undress her for me," Edmund commands, handing a pair of sheers to Nikki before rolling up his sleeves. He wanders the wall beside me, his eyes roaming over the various paddles and whips hanging from many ornate hooks. Lifting a wooden paddle reminiscent of one belonging to an old school ma'am, he directs them, "When you're done, go enjoy each other until we're ready to join you."

Having helped to strip me bare, Nikki catches my attention and gives me a questioning look. I give her a short, silent nod, letting her know that I'm okay.

Still fucking terrified, but I'm too damn curious—or stubborn— to walk away.

Edmund's eyes rake over my body when he returns to me with a black leather flogger and matching paddle in his hands. Every step he takes causes my heart to race faster; fear and anticipation both raging for control.

"Do you know what you signed up for?" He rubs the smooth leather over my ass, alternating between soft and firm strokes.

"Whatever you want." I struggle to push out the words through my panting. I can barely breathe as the leather continues to brush over my skin. Every caress laced with the thrill of knowing it might be the last.

"Good." Quickly, he pulls the flogger back and slaps it against my ass. It hits with a stinging slap, causing me to grunt.

But he doesn't stop.

He swings again and again, placing strikes across my ass and upper thighs. My body clenches with every painful strike, falling lax with a strange euphoria between them.

When he finally pauses, my skin burns from the repeated hits of the flogger. He gingerly places his palm on my warm flesh, rubbing lightly over the marks he left, and I'm suddenly keenly aware of a neediness between my thighs.

Moans and whimpers echo behind me, only furthering my need, and I clench my thighs, trying to provide myself some sort of relief.

"Fuck," Edmund groans as his hand slides up my wet inner thigh, "You're fucking dripping for my pain, aren't you?"

"Yes." I arch my ass into his touch as he swaps the flogger for the paddle.

Standing behind me, he nips along my shoulder and up my neck as he rests the paddle against my pussy. He bites hard on the crook of my neck, and a feral groan rattles from me.

"Did you know you were a dirty little pain slut, Harper?" he whispers against my skin as he rubs the flat of the paddle teasingly between my thighs. It dusts against my pussy, and my hips tremble, wanting to grind against it until I come.

"So fucking needy." He flicks his wrist, and the paddle swats against my pussy.

"Fuuuck," I exhale and suck in the word through my raspy breath as the sting nearly causes me to come.

Edmund gives another light flick before replacing the paddle with his hand. He thrusts two fingers inside of me, and I can't stop myself from grinding down on him.

"This tight little cunt of yours is so fucking wet." He curls his fingers inside of me, and my release builds in the pit of my stomach. He continues to work me hard and fast. My ass grinds against the impressive, hard length in his pants as I ride his hand until I'm panting and moaning for more.

I'm about to come when he pulls his fingers from me, and I groan, "Pleas—"

He shoves his fingers into my mouth, silencing me as he coats my tongue with my own arousal. Firmly, he swats my ass with the paddle, and I grunt around the fingers in my mouth as the sting shoots through me.

"You don't get to come, Harper." As he strikes me again, I greedily suck myself from his fingers. "Not until this perky little ass of yours is the perfect rosy red."

CHAPTER
SEVEN

EDMUND

Liz fucking outdid herself with this one. I've had scores of women attempt to fake their ability to handle what I want to give them. Most doing so miserably.

But Harper...

Fuck, she might be perfect.

The way her body reacts to my touch or to the burning sting of my paddle against her already crimson ass. Both make her so fucking excited that her tight little cunt drips with arousal. She's so fucking wet that her thighs are fucking slick with it.

I want to taste it.

To taste her.

Letting the paddle fall to the floor, I lift her cuffs from the wall just long enough to spin her to face me. She's still off-kilter from the quick twist when I secure her back to the wall. I drop to my knees and lift her thigh over my shoulder. Growling as I lick the sweetness of her arousal from her inner thigh, I sink my teeth into the tender flesh when I nearly reach her cunt. Without pulling from my bite, a delightful whimper spills from her lips.

Roughly cleaning her other thigh with my tongue, I leave a trail of teeth marks as I make my way to her delectable cunt. A string of breathy groans pass over her lips. A beautiful serenade of her pleasure and pain.

And fuck, I'm done for.

Slipping her leg off me as I stand, I unhook her cuffs from the wall and hoist her over my shoulder. After carrying her across the room, I drop her on the bed, startling the two blondes thoroughly engrossed in each other.

They waste no time adding Harper to their activities. One quickly claiming her mouth as the other sucks on one of her nipples. Even with the two of them on her, I still command her full attention, and she stares up at me with lust-filled eyes as I strip out of my clothes.

"She's mine," I growl as I climb onto the bed beside the three of them. "Remove your mouths from her. I'll be the only one tasting her tonight."

They both back away from her to make more room for me. Annoyed that they soiled her mouth with the taste of their cunts, I snarl, "If you need something to do with your mouths, you can suck my cock."

Roughly gripping Harper's ass, I pull her over my face and bury myself in her. I lick and suck at her as I swirl my tongue around her clit. My fingers digging into the aching flesh of her ass, hard enough to bruise, I help her grind herself against my face as the blondes slide their lips along my shaft.

I want her to fucking come all over me.

Her hips spasm on my tongue as she works toward the release she so desperately needs. Her breaths are short and rapid, and I know she's close. I draw her clit into my mouth. Sucking hard, I drag my teeth over her clit, and it's her undoing. Screams rattle from her as she convulses on my face. Her hands wrap around the headboard as she continues to endure the firm flicks of my tongue. When I release my tight grip on her ass, she falls against the bed, sated.

Slipping my fingers into the hair of the blonde whose lips are wrapped around my cock, I taunt Harper as she attempts to catch her breath beside me. "I'm not done with you yet, my little pain slut,"

Fisting the hair in my hand, I drag her over the entirety of my length. Forcing myself down her throat, she gags around my violent intrusion, and fuck, does it feel good. I work her soft pink lips up and down my shaft as I stare at Harper. Her lust-filled eyes match my unwavering gaze.

Fuck, she's the one I want to be inside.

Taking the blonde off my cock and shoving her to the side, she gasps for air as I climb from the bed. When I plant my feet on the floor, I grab Harper's ankles and yank her to the edge of the mattress before roughly pulling her to her feet before me.

Undoing one of the cuffs around her wrists, I move her hands behind her back and secure her momentarily freed arms. I press my hand between her shoulders and bend her over the edge of the bed. As I push her onto the mattress, I nuzzle her face between one of the blonde's thighs.

Without hesitation, she licks at the cunt before her. She works the girl beneath her with a skilled finesse. Her tongue swirls, thoroughly pleasing the blonde; I press my tip to her still-dripping entrance and slip inside her with ease.

"You'll be leaving with my handprints on your ass and a sore fucking cunt." Fisting her hair, I press her firmly into the blonde's cunt, and I'm intrigued by the fact she doesn't fight me. But not nearly enough to keep me from driving myself repeatedly into her.

Fucking perfection.

Gripping the cuffs between her wrists, I use them for leverage to take her harder. Driving into her, deep and hard, she groans into the pussy she's eating for me. I roughly spank her ass with my free hand, and she moans as she quivers around my cock. "That's it, show them how much you fucking love my pain. Let them see what a dirty little slut you are for me."

I pull from her and grab a bottle of lube from the bedside table, slathering a generous amount over my cock. Squeezing it over her, I drip the cool liquid down the crack of her ass. She startles as it hits her skin, and it causes her rosy cheeks to clench. I rub my thumb through the lube and massage it around her hole until she relaxes. She tightens for a second when I press the fat tip of my cock against her

tight hole, whimpering as I slowly stretch her to accommodate me.

I'm not a fucking monster.

"Let me in, Harper," I murmur as I rub my hand along her
hip, and the head of my cock presses inside of her. I still for
a minute before sliding into her tight ass until I'm fully
buried inside of her. Panting, as I try to control my need, I
give her a few languid strokes before needing to stop. My
voice is pained and breathy as I grunt, "Use her cunt to
muffle your screams because I'm not going to be gentle."

I couldn't go easy any longer if I fucking tried.

Relentlessly, I slide out and slam my hips against her ass
with a groan—hers and mine. Repeating the hard, deep
thrusts, I fill her with my cock as I riddle her ass and thighs
with my handprints. She comes for me again and again,
loving every fucking second of the ache on her skin and the
pleasure in her ass.

She's too fucking perfect.

I slow my hips, trying to prolong the inevitable, wanting to
stay buried inside her for the rest of the night. Fucking her
and taking in the glorious work of art I'm making of her
scarlet-painted ass. *Perfect and rosy.* But it's too late. I bury
myself inside of her with a feral groan, filling her with my
cum. Pulling out my still spasming cock, I paint a ribbon of
my seed on her thigh.

I slide my hand through the trail of cum running down her
leg. Gathering it on my index and middle fingers, I plunge
one into her cunt and smear it along her walls. Pulling it
from her, I snake my arm under her tits, lift her from the

bed, and pull her to my chest. Wrapping my hand around her throat, I tip her face up to mine.

"My perfect little rose." I slip my fingers into her mouth and rub the remainder of my cum over her tongue. "I want you leaving with my marks on your ass, my cum in all your perfect fucking holes, and the taste of me on your lips."

CHAPTER EIGHT

DETECTIVE MICHALES

When Mia Dillon walked into the precinct to file a report about being sexually assaulted in the Rusty Anchor parking lot, I thought I might finally have my way in to pin something on these rich, arrogant assholes.

Sam.

Rich.

Cocky.

Conceited.

Dark Hair.

Fancy black sports car.

It took me only a few minutes after her interview to know with all certainty that Samuel Millington was the man she was describing. She was going to be *the one*. The piece of the puzzle that finally connected Samuel, Grant Geyer, Edmund

Parker, William Cattaneo, and Elizabeth Beaufort to the string of women disappearing from my formerly quaint small town. Right up until she disappeared in the middle of the night without a fucking trace.

Just like the rest of them.

When I followed Samuel Millington last night, I thought I'd hit the jackpot when I watched him and all of his devious friends arrive at an old estate on the outskirts of town. Sneaking onto the property, I could never have imagined what I would stumble upon.

Hearing screams and peering into the window, I found Edmund Parker in the midst of a foursome. Three women bound in handcuffs devouring each other as though their lives depended on it—*which they probably did*—while he enjoyed all of them.

I've been watching the video I recorded last night. A countless amount of times. On my phone. Then, on my laptop. Over and over for evidence.

Edmund relentlessly pounding into a petite little redhead while shoving her face into the pussy of a blonde. He strikes her already bright red ass as he slams into her, leaving crimson handprints across her flesh. She screams for him repeatedly, but not for him to stop.

She fucking loves the way he fucks her.

Trying to concentrate on the details—instead of the *abhorrent* sexual acts—I take as many notes as I can regarding the women in the video. I watch the video through to the end, then start it over to begin watching the redhead again. And again before turning my attention to the blonde she was servicing. I loop the video on repeat, seeking out details of these women as though it's an obsession.

Because it is.

By the time I finish, I have photos of the redhead and each of the blondes from the video. My notebook has the few additional details I was able to find. Printing everything out, I shove it into an evidence folder and head to the precinct.

They'll have to listen to me now.

I have proof of just how brutal and wicked these monsters are.

At the precinct, I make several copies and distribute them throughout the office to ensure everyone has the photos of these three women.

"Michales? Is there some sort of investigation into the porn industry the rest of us aren't aware of?" Callahan holds one of the photos in the air with an arrogant grin plastered across his face.

"I've been telling all of you—"

"What the fuck, Michales!" the chief yells as he violently yanks the photo out of Callahan's hand. Walking into the office, he snatches up all of the photos I just distributed before shouting, "My office. Now."

Following him, he slams the door behind me when I step into his office. He takes a seat at his desk and tosses my evidence across his desk.

Discarding it like it is trash.

"I ask, you answer," he huffs as his eyes dart between me and the papers strewn across his desk. "Is this Edmund Parker?"

"Yes." I nod confidently, confirming what I discovered last night.

"For the love of Christ, tell me you downloaded it from some self-posting pornography website."

"No, Chief." He shakes his head disappointingly as I answer. "I was following Samuel Millington, and—"

"Shut the fuck up. Right now." He cuts me off abruptly as he stands and slams his hands into the top of his desk. His head hangs as he takes a few deep breaths. Lifting his gaze to mine, his nostrils flare as he continues to berate my detective work over the past couple of weeks. Not stopping until he's demanded both my badge and gun.

"As of now, you're on disciplinary leave," he shakes his head, "and lucky that I'm not arresting you."

Slamming my badge into his hand and my gun onto his desk, I storm toward the door. He barks, "Stay away from them, Michales."

Fat fucking chance.

CHAPTER NINE

EDMUND

Sitting at my desk, I enjoy my morning coffee while reviewing the expansion plans for the development. Survey reports of additional land I am looking to purchase are spread across my desk, and I'm making notes and developmental placement about them. I'm mid-note on Lot 47 when Aubrey lets herself into the model home that houses my office.

I swear to Christ, she dresses like this on purpose.

A white blouse and pencil skirt shouldn't cause my cock to be this hard.

My eyes roam over her body, uncertain where to garner their attention, before settling on the black fuck-me heels she chose to wear today. Making my way up her legs, I find the sleek, black pencil skirt skimming just below her knees. But as I continue to scan up her body, the fabric is stretched tight, trying to accommodate her Marilyn-esque hips and thighs. It's so tight that I can see the outline of the garter straps holding up her hose. The white blouse tucked into her skirt is sheer enough that there is no denying the lacy, black bra she's adorning beneath it.

"Fucking hell," I mutter under my breath, adjusting my cock as she flashes me a smile from the doorway.

"Good morning, Mr. Parker." Her voice is bubbly and chipper as she drops her things at her desk and makes her way to mine. Bending over the desk, putting the ample swell of her cleavage on clear display, she asks, "Are these for the expansion?"

She's hot.

Not bright.

I hear her words, but the majority of my focus is currently down the gaping neckline of her shirt. Diverting my eyes from her pert tits, I meet her eyes and blurt out, "What?"

"The expansion," she repeats herself as she makes her way to her desk across from mine. "Are you trying to figure out where you plan to put everything?"

*I know **exactly** where I want to put something.*

"They will be," I let out a light, annoyed sigh, "once I manage to take care of a little issue holding things up."

Trying to distract myself, I figure it's finally late enough to text Grant. He had left the party by the time I finished with Harper and the blondes, and it's not like him to leave early like that. Plus, Liz vaguely mentioned that he stormed off, almost leaving his cute little blonde plaything behind.

Where the fuck did you run off to last night?

I'm reaching out to that feisty little redhead from last night. She took my flogger like a fucking champ. Even took my cock in her ass and being suffocated from her face being buried in some little blonde bitch's ass.

You would like her.

GRANT
You'll tire of her.

Eventually, we all do.

And?

When I do, I'll get rid of her and replace her with someone else.

What's going on with you?

Liz made it sound like shit got weird but didn't elaborate?

You at the model today?

What the fuck?

Just answer the question.

Of all of us, Grant definitely keeps his cards closest to his chest. The only way you'll ever know what's going on with him or what he's thinking is if he tells you.

Yeah, The Preserves. Trying to fuck this new agent I've got working for me.

Thank fucking God you aren't Samuel.

> I prefer my women screaming voluntarily.

Maybe a little involuntarily, but not in the same ways as Samuel.

> I just went for a run. I'll meet you over there in about an hour.

> Maybe two.

Closing our conversation, I'm about to place the phone on my desk when I decide to reach out to the redhead. Liz reluctantly gave me her number last night, knowing that I would just get Grant to find it for me if she didn't pass it on. I grab the paper from my desk and key it into my phone to send her a good morning text.

> Good morning.

> How's my dirty little pain slut feeling this morning?

I'm about to put my phone down when a reply pops up.

> **HARPER**
> Who is this?

> Now that hurts my feelings, Harper.

> And here I thought I was the first man to send you home with my handprints all over your ass.

> Oh, you were definitely the first, Edmund.

Her first.

I like that...

> I had fun with you last night, little rose.

> I'd like to do it again.

> I'm interested to see just how far I can push you.

> I can hardly sit this morning.

> But was it worth it?

Three little dots appear and disappear repeatedly as she attempts to type her response. Trying to nudge her, I send another.

> Did the sting on your ass make the pleasure in your cunt that much sweeter?

> You liked it, did you?

> Yes...

> If you want to be a pain slut for me again, you have my number, little rose.

Taking a quick picture, I send it to her before placing my phone back on my desk.

In the meantime...

CHAPTER TEN

HARPER

Gingerly, I take a seat at the kitchen island and wince as I shift my weight in an attempt to get comfortable.

My ass cheeks are fucking sore.

"He really did a number on your last night, huh?" Nikki chuckles.

"The handprint I showed you when we got home," I huff, "it's still there. Along with a few bruises from the paddle."

Nikki bends over the counter, plants her forearms on it, and asks, "But you liked it, didn't you?"

I don't answer because I don't know how to.

No one should like that.

"I mean, you can say you didn't." She reaches over and steals my cup of coffee. She takes a generous sip before continuing, "But with how much you came last night, we both know that's a lie."

"Nikki!" I squeal.

"What?" She shrugs. "You were moaning into my pussy every time he made you come. It was kind of hard not to notice when you hit double digits."

"Nikki!" I exclaim again, my tone a mixture of annoyance and embarrassment.

"It's just sex, Harp," she mumbles as she grabs her own cup of coffee. "It doesn't have to mean anything. It **can** just be fun."

I keep telling myself that, but my brain doesn't seem to get the memo.

Feelings.

There are always fucking feelings. Guilt. Shame. Affection. Heartbreak. While I've had my fair share of sex, there are always feelings.

My phone buzzes with another text message from across the speckled countertop . Swiping it open, I'm met with a picture of his hand. Quickly followed with another text.

> In case you miss me.

"He's a cocky bastard," I huff. "I'll definitely give him that."

"Who's a cocky bastard?" Nikki's eyes light up as she tries to swipe the phone from my hand.

"Edmund."

"He fucking text you?" She holds her hand out for the phone again, and I reluctantly give it to her. She reads through the short exchange of messages before continuing. "Holy shit, Harp. What are you going to say?"

"I don't know..." My voice trails off as I stare into the cooling coffee before me.

"Don't wait too long to get back to him." She passes me back my phone. "Men like him don't exactly wait around. We can talk about this later, but I'm off to see Gerald and blow another month of rent out of him."

"Jesus, Nik," I exhale, but my words don't faze her as she walks out of the front door.

After dumping the last of my coffee down the kitchen sink and placing my cup in the dishwasher, I pick my laptop up and head to the couch. I hope the soft cushions will be more forgiving than the firm barstool, quickly finding it only slightly less painful as I sit.

"Why would I want to see him again?" I huff to myself as I scrunch my face in discomfort while trying to find a comfortable position. Giving up, I wind up sprawled across the couch on my stomach with my chin propped on my hand.

Opening the laptop, my fingers hover against the keys while I debate what I want to look up first.

Men who like to inflict pain during sex.

On website after website, I find the same thing.

Edmund is a sadist.

Sadists get off on inflicting physical or emotional pain on another person. Based on the current state of my ass, I'm going to assume Edmund's interests are physical.

But that isn't the revelation that leads me down a BDSM rabbit hole for hours.

BDSM.

Bondage. Discipline. Sadism. Masochism.

Masochists.

Masochists derive pleasure and sexual gratification from the act of receiving pain.

Am I a fucking masochist?

While I am definitely not loving the current state of my ass, I cannot deny how much I loved every second of it last night.

The sting.

The thud.

The burn.

The blissful fucking burn.

How it hurt...so good.

The way it heightened every one of my senses, making the pleasure he provided that much better.

After taking a minute to think, I pick up my phone and quickly type out a text, hitting send before chickening out.

"Fuck," I whisper under my breath.

CHAPTER ELEVEN

EDMUND

"The landscapers are coming to trim the bushes along the model and some of the properties today. How do you want them?" Aubrey calls from the great room of the model home. Turning toward her voice, I find her bent over the pool table, racking the billiard balls.

"What?" I snap as I stand from my chair, having truly not heard her question with my focus on her ass.

"A little distracted today?" she jokingly snarks as she glances at me over her shoulder. "The bushes. How do you want them trimmed?"

"Bare." My tone is a deep whisper as I step behind her and place my palms on the green felt, boxing her in. Reeling from the high of the fiery redhead and feeling more brazen than usual, I ask, "How do you keep your bush?"

"Mr. Parker!" she exclaims, standing abruptly and finding herself pinned between me and the hardwood of the pool table.

"Aubrey." I speak her name slowly and authoritatively, relishing in the way it causes her breath to hitch. "How long are we going to play this game?"

"What game?" Her voice cracks, and she swallows hard.

"You. Parading around here with your huge tits and round ass on display. Taunting me. Teasing me. As you flirt with me relentlessly day after day."

"I don—"

"Don't play coy with me, Aubrey." I lean forward and press my hardening cock against her ass. "You can pretend to be sweet and innocent, but we both know you want my cock."

Grabbing her hand, I pull it behind her back and place her palm against the bulge in my pants. She gasps as her fingers instinctually wrap around it.

Not so fucking innocent after all.

"We shouldn't," she says softly as she continues to stroke over my length through my trousers. "You're my boss."

"Yes," I groan as her fingers slide over my tip. Gripping her skirt at her thighs, I begin to gather the fabric into my hands, slowly inching it up her legs. With the hemline resting just below her ass, I whisper against the back of her neck, "I am your boss."

"That's why we shouldn—" She catches her words as I slide my hand between her legs and rub against her damp panties.

"Then why are you wet and stroking my cock?" I hoist the skirt over her ass. I reach around her body and begin to undo each of the buttons of her blouse. "Say no. Tell me you don't want to know what it's like to be the naughty girl who fucks her boss. Or say yes. And I can promise I'll fuck you like you've never been fucked before."

She swallows hard, audibly hard, before quietly responding, "Yes."

Pulling the blouse from her, I toss it haphazardly to the floor before yanking the lacy cups of her bra down to expose her massive tits. I roughly palm them both, squeezing and kneading at them as she grinds her ass against my cock. I firmly roll both her tight nipples between my fingers and pull on them, causing her to moan.

"Bend over. Hands on the table. Feet spread," I command, undoing my pants and freeing my aching cock. Without warning, I bring my hand down hard against her ass. Hitting her with such force, her cheeks and thighs jiggle. I smack her other cheek, and the slap of her skin echoes around the room. Her reactions completely devoid of enjoyment, unlike the little redhead I can't stop thinking about.

"Ed—" She attempts to interject my strikes but finds her words cut short with another strike of my palm.

I rub my hand over her pinkened flesh as I slip my fingers beneath the lace of her panties. Gripping the thin string running along her hip, I tug firmly, causing it to tear from the lace and providing me unfettered access to her— *completely unlandscaped*—cunt. I shove into her as my fingers grip the meaty flesh of her hips. Squeezing hard, I use my grip to help drag her over my cock as I slam into her.

She cries out breathlessly through every one of my thrusts into her, pained yelps spewing from her lips with every strike of my palm. I slap against her crimson-marbled skin again, and her slick cunt quivers around my cock as I groan, "Don't fight it, Aubrey. You can like it. Like the dirty little whore we both know you are."

Unable to hold back, she claws at the table and clenches around my cock as she comes. I riddle her ass with hand-prints as she rides out the last of her euphoria. Her cunt still quivering around me, I grunt through my thrusts, "Fuck. I'm going to cover this perfectly marked ass with my cum."

She startles beneath me. Momentarily, I contemplate the fact that the part of what we're doing that repulses her the most is me coming on her—until I see Grant walking through the front door. Aubrey struggles to push herself from the table, but I'm not about to be denied the release I'm so close to after so graciously letting her come.

Gripping her hair, I shove her back against the table. Her face hits the felt and rattles the billiard balls, and I continue to slam my hip as I snarl, "Don't you fucking dare. You're going to take my fucking cock until I'm finished. You're going to let him watch, like the dirty fucking whore you are, as I cover you with my cum. And if he wants to fuck that pretty mouth of yours, you'll take him down your throat like a good little cum slut."

"I'll pass." Grant catches me by surprise as he takes a seat in a large, upholstered chair.

"But I'm more than open to seeing what a good little whore she is," he taunts. "Do you like being used? Or do you hate the enjoyment you get from being someone's whore?"

She fucking hates it.

For as long as I've waited to fuck her, this is quite a lackluster fuck.

Pressing a palm to her back and holding her on the table, her face rubs against the felt as I continue to pound into her. "Eyes on Grant," I growl. "Give him the pleasure of watching your loathing, self-disgust for enjoying how I treat you."

Staring at Grant, with tears welling in her eyes, she takes every brutal thrust of my cock until I force her to come for me again. Quickly pulling from her, I take matters into my own hands and vigorously fist my cock. Closing my eyes, that feisty redhead flashes through my thoughts, and I groan as my cum splatters across Aubrey's ass.

My hand smacks her tender ass, and I smear my seed over her skin before using the remnants of her panties to clean up before tucking myself back into my pants and pulling her skirt back over her hips. Handing her shirt from the floor, I send her to get herself together and meet some clients who are arriving in a few minutes.

"Sweetheart," I call after her, "If you want more of my cock or miss my sting on your ass, you know where to find me."

She won't.

And that's fine.

CHAPTER TWELVE

HARPER

There's a knock at the front door to our apartment, and a moment later, Nikki shouts, "Harp, it's for you."

Taking my time walking from my room, I'm surprised to find her standing at the island with a small red box in her hand.

"I'm not expecting anything." I shake my head as I take the surprisingly hefty box from her.

"I kind of think that's the point," she chuckles.

I lift the tag dangling from the perfectly tied black bow and read it out loud.

For your perfectly-marked perky little ass.

If you need help rubbing it in, give me a call.

"Well, at least you know the box is way too small for it to be a dildo," she snickers.

I mean, I guess she's right.

After placing it on the counter, I pull the satin bow, and ribbons pool around the box. Lifting the lid, I find a cute little apothecary jar. I take it out and read the label: *Arnica Cream* and put it on the counter.

"What the hell is arnica cream?"

Nikki quickly swipes her thumbs across the screen of her phone and says, "Arnica cream is topically used for bruises and muscle aches. It stimulates circulation and healing."

"Am I supposed to send a thank you for ass cream?" I quip with a hint of sincerity. "Do you think it works?"

"Based on how carefully you're still sitting this afternoon, I kind of think it won't hurt," she tries to control her snicker. "Maybe you should take him up on the application offer."

"Absolutely not." I swipe the jar off the counter and head to my bathroom to apply it to my tender ass in privacy.

I'm washing the excess cream off my hands when my phone buzzes.

> **EDMUND**
> What? No thank you?

> I haven't been able to sit since last night.

> And you want me to thank you?

> Was I too hard on you, little rose?

> Maybe this will help.

As if on cue, there's another knock at the door. So help me if he's standing on the other side, and I'm unshowered in frumpy sweats and a messy bun. Pulling open the door, I'm met with a courier holding a red gift box. This one is substantially larger than the last. When I take it from him, it's also surprisingly lighter.

"Thank you." I tip my head as I push the door shut with my feet.

"Another one?" Nikki pops her head over the back of the couch. "What's the tag say?"

"To ensure you're ready for Saturday. E."

"I'm sorry?" Nik nearly jumps from the couch. "Did you forget to tell me you said yes to him?"

"I sent him a text after you left this morning. I didn't exactly say *yes*, just that I might be interested."

He apparently took that as an enthusiastic yes.

Undoing the ribbon, I lift the lid to find an anal plug sitting atop the perfectly folded tissue paper. A quite large one at that. Nikki must notice the look on my face because she jests, "Harp, if you could take his cock, that thing is going to be a piece of cake."

She's not wrong.

I've never taken anything as large as him, and quite frankly, while I prepped for the evening, I'm still not entirely sure how he managed with such ease.

Pulling back the tissue paper, I find a luxurious black and pink lace panty-set with a matching garter and hose. Under that is a black Valentina midi-dress with a slit up the thigh, which looks like it will leave very little to the imagination.

"I need a minute." Rushing, I grab everything and take it to my room, shutting the door to get a few minutes of privacy.

> I didn't say yes.

Maybe not in those exact words.

But I believe your text said…

I'm interested. Can we talk?

This asshole really just copied and pasted my text to him from earlier.

> Talk.

> Not go out on a date.

> Definitely not fuck you again.

You don't know it yet, but you will be fucking me again.

> I need to know now, is that all you want from me?

> Because I'm not interested in just being someone's little fuck toy.

If you're looking for someone to love and cherish you, I'm not your guy.

We can have some fun. Enjoy each other's company.

You can explore that little pain slut hiding inside of you.

There's that phrase again...

Just dinner.

No expectations.

Saturday.

Just dinner.

To talk.

But wear the gifts.

You might be surprised at how charming
I am.

CHAPTER
THIRTEEN

EDMUND

"Fuck!" I angrily shout, tossing my gin and tonic across the room. It hits the wall, causing the glass to shatter. Ice clatters against the floor as the remains of my beverage drip down the navy blue wall.

My request with the city council to expand The Preserves beyond the current zoned area was denied yet again. Something about Mr. Marshall wanting to protect the wetlands at the tail edge of the area I'm looking to begin construction on.

When I purchased it six months ago, I had been not so subtly informed by other members of the council that there would *be ways* to ensure my request would go through without a hitch.

They apparently had not spoken with Mr. Marshall.

Three requests now. All of them have been stalemated for fear of "disrupting the animal habitats and possible shoreline erosion."

Unlike his cohorts, Mr. Marshall isn't open to *persuasion*. He has been unwilling to discuss the matters with me. Or my bank account. And the asshole is as clean as a fucking whistle. The worst I could blackmail him with would be parking too far from the curb when he stopped at Latte Da yesterday morning on his way to the office.

Since he's too good for bribes and way too fucking clean for blackmail, there seems to be only one other solution to my problem.

On the plus side, he's so squeaky fucking clean that I know exactly where to find him this evening. The Adelaide Cove Food Pantry. As the director, I'm banking on the fact that he'll be the last to leave and lock up as everyone else starts filing out for the night.

He steps through the door with one other volunteer. They make their quick goodbyes, and he's at the door alone as she slips into an awaiting car.

People can be so fucking predictable.

Silently slipping from my car, I make my way across the street and begin walking toward him.

"Mr. Parker?" A look of confusion washes over his face when he sees me.

"Mr. Marshall." I nod. "I'd like a minute of your time."

"I've made it very clear that I am not interested in discussing this matter with you." He begins to pick up his pace in an attempt to walk away from me.

"Yes, your assistant has made that more than clear." I keep his pace with ease. "Unfortunately, I'm a fucking stubborn man who's very used to getting exactly what he wants."

"I'm sorry," he shakes his head, "but you aren't getting what you want. I will not concede on this matter. I'll protect those wetlands with my life."

"I thought that's what you'd say." I shake my head.

Reaching his car, he fumbles with the key fob, desperately trying to unlock the door. As he struggles, I take a brief look around to ensure we are alone as I pull a folding knife from my pocket.

He pulls at the car door as I flip the blade open. Gripping the shirt at the center of his back, I throw him into the door with a thud and slam it shut before plunging the knife into his back. He opens his mouth to scream but only gurgles blood as I shove the knife into his chest for a second time. The two will be more than enough to be fatal, but I jam the knife into him one more time simply for being a pain in my ass.

Holding him upright as he gasps for air unsuccessfully, I reach into his pants pockets for his wallet. He crumbles to the ground, eyes wide as he watches me rummage through to see what I can take.

Sixty-four dollars.

I shove the money into my pocket and drop the leather wallet on the ground beside him. Squatting down, I wipe the bloody blade across his shirt to clean it. With a sense of satisfaction, I watch the light quickly diminish from his eyes, I tuck the knife back into my pocket.

"You probably should've taken the fucking money." Condescendingly, I pat his cheek as he struggles to take his last breath.

Rising to my feet, I pull off my gloves and make my way back to my car. The streetlight hits the face of my watch, and I glance at it. Done much sooner than expected.

Plenty of time to get across town for my Chinese takeout.

CHAPTER
FOURTEEN

EDMUND

Being swamped at the new builds—and taking care of my now-passed zoning request issue—for the past couple of days, I left my new assistant in charge of making reservations for my night—or nights—with Harper. Looking over the itinerary she handed me before leaving at noon, she did a remarkable job.

Travel arrangements, dinner reservations at Delilah, and the penthouse suite at the Bellagio. A suite I fully intend to use.

Leaving the office, I head home and quickly pack my bag. My primary focus is on restraints, a Wartenberg wheel, an e-stim wand with a few attachments, and a gag. Finally content with my toys for our trip, I hop in the shower to quickly clean up.

Rinsing my hair and lathering the soap over my body, it becomes quite apparent that my cock has other intentions than a quick rinse. It's hard—*painfully so*—at the mere thought of the things I plan to do to Harper this evening.

I haven't come in the last thirty-six hours, and I waste no time wrapping my hand around my shaft. My thoughts immediately drift to Harper.

Her hands and feet bound securely to my bench as she's bent over it with her ass and cunt on full display for me. Standing behind her, I stroke my cock as she struggles to stay on her tiptoes to alleviate the strong vibration of the wand situated between her thighs. Her whole body trembles as she suffers through orgasm after orgasm.

My hand slides along my length, from base to tip, direly wishing it were inside of her instead.

"Please..." Her words quivering as much as her body. "I can't."

"You can. And you will." I firmly slap my palm against her ass before slipping inside of her. Gripping her hips, I push her hard against the bench, forcing her to take the brunt of the wand vibrating against her clit as I pound against her ass.

Picking up my pace, I vigorously fist my cock. Desperately needing to come.

Her ass shakes against my hips, and the strong vibrations of the wand travel along my cock. It's so fucking perfect that I fight the urge—no, the need—to fill her. But when she comes again, with a primal scream as her cunt violently spasms around me, I'm done for.

My cock stiffens, and my firm grip twitches as cum shoots from my tip and is washed down the drain.

"Fuck…" I breathe out as I continue to leisurely stroke my sensitive shaft and shut off the water. I have fantasized about plenty of women with my hand wrapped around my cock, but never about one I've already been inside of.

But Harper…

I can't stop thinking about her.

I've been telling myself all week that it doesn't mean anything. Well, anything other than she was a fantastic fuck toy that I want to enjoy again.

My shower took longer than expected, as confirmed by a quick glance at my Rolex. The car service will be arriving any minute. Quickly drying, I head to the walk-in closet and throw on a suit before grabbing my bag of supplies and heading downstairs to meet the driver.

————

> I'm about ten minutes away.

> I'll come up to get you, be sure you're ready.

> We have dinner reservations to get to.

HARPER
You DO know it's still lunchtime, right?

> Are you questioning me, Harper?

> Be ready.

Dots come and go for a moment, but the response I get would've only taken her a second to type and send.

K

We come to a stop outside a luxury apartment complex. One far too nice for Harper to be able to afford. She may have made enough money to rent this place last week, but there's no way they would've had a vacancy that quickly. This is one of the most sought-after buildings in the city. I'm only more intrigued—*or perplexed*—when security gives me directions to her apartment. It's not the penthouse, but it's still half the floor.

Knocking on the door, I'm pleased to find Harper ready to go. She gently nudges me out of the way and steps into the hallway. "I would invite you in, but my roommate has company over."

"Understood." I slip my hand against the small of her back and lead her toward the elevator. My hand lingers just above her ass as we ride down to the lobby.

Stepping from the building and onto the street, I motion toward the Town Car.

"I expected you to be more of a flashy sports car kind of guy." She smiles up at me as she slides across the backseat.

"I am." I smirk at her astute observation of me.

We ride in silence for the majority of our short ride to the airfield. My eyes repeatedly roam over her body, wondering if she's wearing the lacy undergarments I hand-picked for her under the vintage Valentina dress Erin purchased. Or if the plug is tucked snugly in her ass.

"So, Edmund." she breaks the silence. "Why are you rushing me out of the door before one in the afternoon for a dinner date?"

Perfect timing.

We pull to a stop on the tarmac, and I open the door, exposing the private aircraft needed to take us to dinner. Extending my hand, she tentatively slips hers into it before climbing out of the car.

"Where are we going?" she asks timidly.

"Delilah's."

"And that's where?"

"Vegas."

"Before I get on that plane, I'm going to text my roommate and tell her where you're taking me."

And she's smart, too.

Not too smart, though; she's still planning to get on the plane.

CHAPTER FIFTEEN

HARPER

This is absurd.

One hundred percent not real life.

*People do **not** actually live like this.*

I'm in complete awe when I take the last of the steps into the plane. It's lavish. Fully decorated in dark wood and cream linens. It looks nothing like any plane I've been on in my life, flying coach rubbing arms and thighs with the people seated next to you.

"Champagne?" The flight attendant extends an already-poured glass toward me, and I hesitate to take it.

"Go ahead," Edmund grants me the permission I didn't realize I was waiting for. "Just go easy."

I take a small sip, heeding what was definitely a warning, and I take a seat on the plush cream sofa. Suddenly acutely aware of the plug in my ass, I shift my weight on the couch.

Edmund sits beside me, close enough that his pants brush against my calf. My heart begins to race a little faster, only intensifying when the crew shut the plane door.

I'm letting a strange man fly me across the country...

"You aren't going to kill me and bury me in the desert, are you?" My nerves get the better of me, and the words blurt from my mouth.

"No." He cracks a smile. "There are way too many animals in the desert. Encased in concrete is the way to go."

"Wow," I laugh and take another sip of my champagne. "And I thought I watched a lot of true crime television."

"Harper. I'm curious." He shifts on the couch so that he's facing me. "Your apartment—"

"I know." I roll my eyes. "It's absurd. But Nikki lets me live there with her practically for free."

"So, she comes from a family with money?"

"Um," I stall, trying to carefully word my answer. "She has a few wealthy Daddies."

"And you?"

"Do I have a Daddy? No, definitely not." I begin to ramble. "The other night. That was a one-time thing for me. Nik talked me into it, but that's it for me."

"And why's that?"

"I can handle what happened in Adelaide Cove. It was a transaction. No false pretenses." I take another sip from my flute. "What she does...it's too much acting. Too much pretend."

"Interesting." He places his hand on my knee, and my thighs clench involuntarily. "You intrigue me, Harper."

You fucking intrigue the hell out of me, too, Edmund Parker.

"Is that what you're looking for?" I ask sincerely.

"A Daddy?" he jests.

"No, silly," I laugh. "To be someone's Daddy? I mean, you are almost twenty years older than me."

"I lack the ability to care and nurture required to be a Daddy." His hand slides along my thigh.

"But here you are, flying me across the country for dinner."

"One of the best beef wellingtons you'll ever have."

My hand lingers over his on my leg as I ask, "And what else do you have planned for us this evening?"

"That depends entirely on you, little rose."

His hand stays on me the rest of the flight—my knee, my thigh, the side of my face, but not once does he leave me for more than a mere second—as we continue to talk and get to know more about each other.

By the time we land, I'm thinking back on his text the other day. *You might be surprised at how charming I am.*

At our first meeting, I was nervous as hell. We barely exchanged names before he was deep inside me. And not a word was spoken between us after either.

But tonight, we've talked non-stop for the entirety of our four-hour flight and the subsequent drive to dinner. I have no nerves about what I want. *And it isn't dinner.* I'm currently dying to have his hands on me again. It's the only thing I can think about.

"Edmund." I place my hand over his as he pulls to a stop at the valet of the restaurant, causing him to immediately turn to look at me. "Did you get us a hotel room?"

"Yes." His response is flat and factual.

"I'd rather have room service."

CHAPTER
SIXTEEN

HARPER

Walking into the penthouse suite at the Bellagio, I'm suddenly second-guessing my choice to hop back into bed with Edmund.

Or at least having second thoughts about him tenderizing my ass again.

Staring out of the window, overlooking the fountain below, I try to reel in my thoughts. Edmund steps behind me, and I flinch when his knuckles drag along the bare skin of my upper arm.

"Nervous?" He spins me around and swiftly pins me to the cool sheet of glass before lifting my hands above my head.

"A little." I swallow hard.

"Don't be." He wraps his hand around my throat and tips my face up toward his. Dipping his head, he presses his lips to mine for the first time. They are soft and supple, and I already know I'm going to miss the feel of them.

With one hand firmly around my throat and the other pinning me to the glass, his tongue slips between my lips. He massages his tongue against mine, claiming my mouth with a silent confidence until I'm moaning into him.

Pulling back, he nips at my lower lip. His bite has such force that I can't help but lick it to make sure he didn't draw blood. He's hovering so close that my tongue drags along his lip as well, causing him to let out a light growl.

"I want to push you." His lips vibrate against mine as he speaks. "Do you want to see how far you can go?"

I shake my head lightly.

"If you want to know the heights to which my pain can take you, you need to use your words. While you still can."

"Yes," I muster my response as I hang on to his final words.

"That's a good girl." Edmund loosens his hands on me before roughly spinning me and pushing me face-first to the glass. His fingers are immediately on the zipper of my dress, and he takes his time drawing it down my spine. Every breath he takes expels his warmth across the now bare skin of my back, eliciting goosebumps.

Reaching the base of the zipper, he slips his warm hands between the slit in the fabric. His fingers travel up my spine and across my shoulders, setting my skin on fire as he lets the dress fall down my arms. It slides down my body, quickly pooling at my feet. Smoothing his hands over my skin, he follows the same path of my dress until he's kneeling behind me, and his hands are resting on my thighs.

He lifts my feet, taking them out of the pool of fabric and spreading my legs wide. My heart races in anticipation— and a little fear—of what is to come.

"Look at you." He runs his hands along the strap of my garter as he retakes his place standing behind me. "Pressed against the glass for everyone to see. Do you think they know what a little whore you're going to be for me? Or do you think we need to show them?"

He doesn't give me a chance to answer. His hand presses firmly between my shoulders, shoving my face and bra-covered breasts against the icy glass as his fingers slide inside me. His hand slides up my neck, and his fingers tangle in my hair as he wraps it around his fist. He vigorously thrusts and curls his fingers, demanding my orgasm. He nips at my neck, pulling at my hair until my scalp burns as he deeply whispers, "This one will be easy, but you're going to *earn* the rest of them."

Easy?

The pain radiating around my crown only accentuates the pleasure building from his skillful touch in my pussy. My nails claw at the pane of glass before me, needing to cling desperately to something as my release begins to build in my core. It shoots through me, and my screams fog over the glass as my knees buckle .

"Hands and forehead on the glass, Harper," Edmund commands as he slips his fingers out of me and pulls my panties back in place. "Do not move."

The hard soles of his shoes click against the marble floor, moving away from me and then slowly returning. Stopping a few feet behind me, he stands silently for what feels like an eternity before instructing, "Hands down, face on the glass."

Lowering my hands to my sides, he undoes the clasp of my bra. Quickly sliding it down my sides, he discards it to the floor.

"Hands back on the glass." His voice is deep and gravelly. "We'll start off light. This is a Wartenberg wheel."

He places it on the back of my hand. Lightly rolling it down my arm, it leaves a sharp, tickling sensation in its wake.

This is nothing like the other night.

"Like any of my toys, it can be light..." He rolls it over my hip and along the edge of my panties. Reaching the fleshy part of my thigh, he increases the pressure, causing each tine of the wheel to feel like a tiny bite. "Or it can hurt."

I wince at the tiny, sharp pains as he drags the wheel back over my hip and along my back. Flexing my fingers against the glass, my back arches from the sensation as I let out a deep, garbled breath.

"You like the bite," he presses hard as he rolls it over my ass and down my thigh, causing me to yelp, "don't you?"

"Yes." My response is quick and breathy.

CHAPTER
SEVENTEEN

EDMUND

"We're going to go harder." I slip a hand between her and the glass, showing her the gag. "I'm going to trust that I don't need this to silence you. If you scream too loudly, I will need to gag you. Understood?"

"Mhmm," she mutters, nodding against the glass.

"This is going to bite." I tap the violet wand against her ass, just long enough for the electricity to arch through her body. She winces and jerks her body away from the sharp sting.

"Breathe, little rose," I remind her when she continues to hold her breath. She lets out a heavy gasp and sucks in a breath as I tap against her other cheek, causing her to flinch. Lowering the sensitivity, I place the prong against her calf and teasingly drag it up her thigh. Her leg trembles, and she lets out a pleasing moan that travels straight to my cock.

Repeating the motion up her other leg, I press my hand between her thighs. While not surprised, I am pleased to find her panties already soaked. Pulling them to the side, I push a finger inside her. I turn up the wand—to a sharp bite of a setting—and repeatedly tap it against her ass until she's struggling to breathe. Thrusting my fingers in and out, I place my lips against the back of her ear before whispering, "Show me how much you like the pain."

Her ass spasms from the repeated surge of shocks coursing through her. Cracked moans and screams vibrate over her lips as she begins to quiver around my fingers buried in her. She grinds her hips against my hand, needing desperately to come. Crying out as she finally falls over the edge, her release trickles down my hand as she nearly crumples against the glass.

Scooping her satiated body into my arms, I carry her to the bed and lay her on it. I strip from my clothes as her eyelids grow heavy. I run my hand along her leg as I climb onto the bed. "Not yet, little rose. I still plan to mark you and see what it feels like to come inside this tight little cunt of yours."

I climb between her thighs on my knees, tuck her legs, and fold them both around my left hip. Pulling her panties to the side, I press the tip of my cock against her glistening entrance. Gripping her thigh and ass, I drive into her until I'm buried to the hilt.

Fuck, she feels even better than I remember.

Lifting my hand, I bring it down hard against her ass as I slam into her, relishing in the bliss that washes over her face. It's almost as pleasurable as the scarlet handprint just left on her smooth, porcelain skin. Both only fuel my need, and I drive into her hard and deep. I watch her tits bounce with every savage thrust as I leave my marks across her ass.

Breathy moans rattle from her, drawing my attention to her pouty pink lips, leaving me with the strange need to feel them as I unload myself into her.

Claiming her.

...as mine.

Spanking her one more time, I lean forward and wrap my fingers around her throat. Her heavy eyes meet mine as I linger over her and bring myself toward the lips I need to taste. They part slightly when my own brush against them, and I waste no time pressing my tongue between them.

Our tongues wrestle, and her fingers slide into my hair. Her gesture is so soft and tender in comparison to the violent way I'm taking her cunt and roughly kneading the perky tit in my hand.

Her back arches from the bed, pressing her chest against mine as it heaves with each of her heavy breaths. Her breaths match my grunts and thrusts, our bodies fighting to keep meeting each other's needs. She comes around my cock as her moans of pleasure fill my mouth. Pulling from our kiss, my lips travel down her neck and suck hard at her collarbone—painfully hard, judging by her nails currently clawing my back.

I'm not into receiving pain, but fuck, I love the way she reacts to me.

"Fuck," I kiss over her already bruising flesh. "I want to mark every fucking inch of you."

"Please..." she begs with such need I almost think she might perish if I don't.

"Don't tempt me." I suck the meaty part of her breast into my mouth and bite. Hard. She screams in pain when the pleasure of her orgasm explodes through her body, tearing her nails through the flesh of my back.

"Fuck!" I growl between her tits. Violently working my hips, I race toward my own release. Slamming into her a final time, I press my lips against hers as my cock spasms inside of her, filling her with my cum.

Pulling from her, I continue to taste her lips until she's too far away to reach them as I settle onto the bed next to her. Rolling her to her side, I nestle in behind her and pull her sluggish body against me.

"You did so fucking good for me, little rose." I rub my lips along the curvature of her neck as her breathing begins to slow, sleep quickly taking the place of her exhaustion. "I can't stop thinking about the things I want to do to you... with you."

Fuck.

This isn't like me.

CHAPTER EIGHTEEN

HARPER

A warm hand lingering up and down my spine rouses me from my sleep. Waking up, I find myself tangled in Edmund. My head on his chest, both our arms and legs wrapped around each other.

"You don't strike me as the cuddly type," I mutter against his chest as my finger traces down the ripples of his stomach.

"I'm not." His hand moves lower until he's cupping my ass. "I haven't shared my bed with a woman in years."

Before I can say a word, he swiftly rolls us both and pushes me face-down onto the mattress. His fingers slide up my spine and into my hair. He fists it roughly and yanks my head back, and I can't help but smile as a moan rattles from me.

"It was the only way I could ensure I got to fuck you again this morning," Edmund groans as his lips and teeth travel along my exposed neck. He rubs his cock teasingly along my entrance before slipping himself inside. Still tender from last night, I groan at his intrusion.

"Are you sore, little rose?" His voice is soft as tender words are whispered against my neck while he begins to savagely thrust against my ass. "Too bad, because I don't intend to be gentle with you."

And he's not.

Not that I even remotely expect him to be.

He likes it to hurt.

We both do...

He takes me hard and fast, setting my pussy on fire. My screams and cries are muffled by the pillow my face presses into as he peppers my ass with his hands.

Fuck, he feels good.

Edmund slams into me, burying himself ungodly deep as I come around him, causing my entire body to tremble with bliss. His hands knead the already aching skin of my ass, and he lets out a roar as he comes inside of me.

Edmund stays deep inside of me as his sweaty body collapses half on top of me. Using his grip on my hair, he pulls my mouth to his and kisses me—*matching my need*—claiming my mouth as rough and hard as he just took my pussy.

"I want to keep you here," his lips rest against mine, "and fuck you until you're unable to walk, but I have business to get back to tonight."

Pulling up to my building, Edmund helps me out of the car. I take a small step from him, and he roughly pulls me back to him, immediately wrapping his fingers around my throat. He tips my face up toward his and stares down at me with a heated, unwavering gaze.

He presses his lips against mine and wraps his arm around my body, pulling me possessively tight against him. His kiss is demanding. It and the tight hold on my throat quickly making me breathless. Every bit of the roughness behind it travels straight between my thighs.

If the intention is to leave me wanting more from him, it's working.

Pulling back from our kiss but keeping my lip between his teeth, he stares at me for a moment before speaking. "I intend to see you again, little rose."

I don't think I could say no if I tried.

Heading inside, my legs feel unsteady, like they belong to a newborn deer. I step into the elevator, already missing the feel of his lips on mine, and my fingers linger over my swollen lips.

Opening the apartment door, the look on Nikki's face shatters my high. I've known her far too long; something isn't right. She looks downright broken.

"Nik?" I quickly cross the room to her. "What's wrong?"

"I'm so sorry," she sobs. "I never should've convinced you to go to that party. It's not your scene. And now..."

"And now, what?"

She proceeds to give me the play-by-play of her date last night, which turned out to be a cop. A disgusting, dirty cop who is now blackmailing her for sex to prevent a video of that first night with Edmund from being leaked to everyone in her life.

"My family can't find out..." she exhales.

"And mine can?" I shriek. She's had hours to come to terms with this situation. I've had minutes, and my emotions are all over the place. "I want to see it."

"Trust me, it's bad."

"I said, I want to see it."

She pulls out her phone and sends a message through an app.

> I talked to Harper.

> **Blackmailing Asshole**
> What did she say?

> She wants to see the video.

> Give me your cell phone number.

She sends her number, and a moment later she receives a single text of a video clip. Taking the phone from her, I press play. I watch for a minute before tossing the phone in her lap and burying my face in my hands.

"Whatever he wants," I mumble as I shake my head. "Until I figure out how to make this go away."

> She said she'll do whatever you want.

> I'm going to need to hear it from her.

Mere seconds later, a FaceTime call pops on the screen. Nikki hands me the phone, and I open to find a very normal-looking middle-aged man. Holding back tears— and the urge to scream at him—I give him the statement he needs, "Like Nikki said, that video can't get out. I'll give you everything she offered."

"What kind of confirmation are you going to give on that?" His words cause bile to rise in my throat.

"Well, I can't exactly suck you off over the phone now, can I?" I snark.

"I'm going to need something," he continues to press. "I need you to take a little initiative like your friend, Nikki, and tell me a bit about what is happening in this video."

"I'm getting fucking railed while eating out my roommate." I close my eyes as I exhale the salty words. "Is that what you want to hear?"

"I'm going to need more, Harper." He's relentless, and as much as it disgusts me, I know what he wants.

"Nikki, he wants more."

"Prop the phone on the table," she instructs me as she pulls off her tank top, exposing her breasts. "I'll help you give him what he wants."

Grabbing my hand, she cups it over her breast as she kisses my lips, erasing the feel of Edmund on them. Beyond her on the screen sits a man pulling out his dick and beginning to slide his hand along it.

"Just fake it," Nikki whispers quietly in my ear. "He'll finish quickly, and it'll be over."

She shimmies my skirt up my thighs and spreads my legs, putting me on display for him. I close my eyes as she slides her fingers inside me, unable to see him yet still subject to every sound he makes as he gets off to this. The disgust—at both his noises and my own actions—causes bile to rise in my throat as Nikki continues to rub between my thighs.

It'll be over quickly...

CHAPTER
NINETEEN

EDMUND

Pulling into the estate, it appears that no one else has arrived for our emergency meeting regarding Detective Asshole and his snooping around one of the girls I apparently recently partied with. Grant pulls in as I climb from my Lotus.

"My cock is like one of Pavlov's fucking dogs," I call to him as he opens his car door. "He gets all excited as soon as I see this place."

"It's a business night. Keep your cock in your pants," he huffs. "And far away from me."

Grabbing my awaiting gin and tonic as we pass through the entryway, Grant and I head straight to our makeshift boardroom.

"Nikki should be arriving in a few minutes. Are we all up to speed so far?" Liz questions over the side conversations occurring around the room.

The bell rings for the front door, and a few moments later, the butler escorts Nikki in. Only it isn't the blonde that I'm assuming is Nikki, who draws my attention.

Why the fuck is Harper standing beside her?

"You were supposed to come alone," Liz scolds the blonde.

"I...I'm sorry," Nikki stutters. "I didn't know how to get back in touch with you. You're going to want to talk to Harper, too, after this morning."

What the fuck happened this morning?

"What were you doing with the man at Nikolai's?" Grant asks.

"I met him through an app that matches men like you to girls like us," Nikki begins, and I glare at Harper. *Like us?* "Only the man that arrived was not the one I was talking to. I was about to bail when he showed me a video."

"A video?" Liz questions.

Nikki pulls her phone from the back pocket of her shorts, opens the video, and slides her phone across the table. Lifting it from the table, the small screen plays a shaky home video of her, Harper, and the other blonde I played with that night. Having seen enough, I pass the phone back to her.

"He threatened to share it with my family and all of UNC if I didn't give him what he wanted."

"And what was that?" Grant questions.

"Sex to keep quiet."

"And you agreed?" Nikki's response piques Liz's interest.

"Yes," Nikki continues. "To a weekly fuck."

She continues to recount the details of the arrangement made between them, right down to how she blew him in the back room at Nikolai's. While she talks, my eyes fixate on Harper. She stands beside Nikki, nervously fidgeting and unable to meet my gaze.

"And Harper?" Liz asks, and I wait for Harper to speak.

Instead, Nikki answers for her, "I messaged him this morning to let him know Harper was on board because he told me he was willing to expose her, too."

The fuck she is.

The sudden swell of possessiveness over her catches me off-guard, and I grip the arms of my chair so hard it hurts as Nikki continues, "He watched us finger each other to prove her agreement, and he's expecting both of us to pay up on Thursday when he comes to our apartment."

"And you're going to give whatever he wants." Liz flashes a cheeky smile at Nikki and Harper. Upon hearing the words, I want to lunge across the table and slap some sense into her.

That is not the answer.

My nostrils flare as I try to control my breathing, pushing down the anger quickly building inside of me.

"You aren't going to do anything?" Harper breaks her silence, and I'm suddenly met with her teary eyes waiting for me to swoop in and save her.

That's not who I am, little rose.

"You get to keep your million dollars." Liz crosses the room and grips Harper's face with such force that her nails dimple her cheeks. "Is that not enough for you, *princess*? Considering you fuck drunk frat boys for flat beer, I'm thinking two grand a week is more than sufficient."

Quickly, Liz's eyes scan over those of us sitting at the table, waiting for disagreement.

Disagreement I know Harper is waiting for.

Disagreement that doesn't come.

"You don't speak a fucking word about the five of us or what happens in this house. You'll zealously take his cock in all your holes. You'll fucking suck his toes while Nikki eats his ass if that's what he wants. Understood?"

"Yes, ma'am," Harper responds as if in pain, but I'm certain her current anguish is from much more than the bruising grip on her jaw.

"We'll be in touch, ladies." I stare at Harper as I speak the words because they're meant for her.

CHAPTER
TWENTY

EDMUND

Taking a deep breath as Harper and Nikki walk from the room, Samuel drops his two cents on the situation. "We should just fucking kill him."

"He's a fucking cop." Will smacks him up the backside of the head. "You can't just kill cops in a small fucking town like this and not expect to be caught."

Spoken like a man with experience.

"They'll give him what he wants," Liz states matter-of-factly as she shrugs her shoulders. "It'll keep him content and quiet for a bit while we figure out how to handle him."

"I hate to agree with the stupid kid on this one, but eliminating the problem really might be the easiest solution," I side with Samuel. "Not immediately, but after enough time that we could pin it on the girls for blackmail."

Getting Harper out of this unscathed—*and untouched by Detective Asshole*—is my top priority for reasons that totally escape me.

"If we go that route, the video gets leaked, Eddie." Liz's displeasure with the idea is clear.

Fuck, I hate when she calls me that.

"Did we watch the same video?" I scoff with a smirk. "An hour-long video of me thoroughly fucking and pleasuring three different women; that's like a fucking dating ad for more pussy than I can fucking handle."

Or want...

Where the fuck did that thought come from?

After a brief discussion regarding security for our compound, Grant's new pet, and the party here on Saturday, we all slowly head our separate ways.

As I step outside, part of me is hoping to find Harper waiting. But she's long gone.

It's not like I've given her any reason to stick around.

Climbing into my car, I slip it into drive and pull away. I pull Harper's contact information up on the dash. I don't press the button to call her. I have so many questions running through my brain, but I don't know where to start.

I need to get my shit straight .

The only woman in my life who wasn't a one-and-done was Chloe, but she didn't mean anything to me—nothing more than a living, breathing fuck doll who lived in my house. She was simply willing holes for me to fuck and an ass for my paddle when and where I saw fit.

Nothing more.

She spent the majority of her time in the east wing of the house, and unless I called for her, we rarely crossed paths. Her feet never even saw inside my master suite. I'd fuck her in a guest bedroom, so I could leave her and retreat to the comfort of my own bed alone when I'd had my fill of her for the evening.

That was how I wanted it.

Nothing like it was with Harper last night. I didn't lie to her. I'm not a cuddler. Actually, never in my life have I cuddled with a woman after sex. But with her, even after I'd finished using her and filling her with cum, I wanted more.

Every time with her, I want more...

More than the sweet suck of her mouth. More than the warmth of her cunt. Even more than the tightness of her ass.

Just, more...

"Jesus, Ed..." I mutter to myself as I pull to a stop in front of my home. "What the fuck is wrong with you?"

Walking inside, I pull my phone from the pocket of my trousers and call Harper. She sends me immediately to voicemail. I call her again, only to get the same response.

> **HARPER**
> I don't want to talk to you.

> I'm not good at taking no for an answer.

Are you okay?

Am I okay????

Are you fucking serious right now?

Watch your mouth with me, Harper.

I don't belong to you.

Her text fucking stings more than I thought mere words could.

And I know we aren't a thing, but you've made it very fucking clear how little I fucking mean to you.

I told you to watch the way you speak to me.

You aren't the boss of me.

I'm done.

I'll take my $2K for my weekly blackmail fuck.

But I'm done.

Done with you.

But I'm not done with you, little rose.

Not even fucking close.

CHAPTER
TWENTY-ONE

HARPER

"The fucking audacity." I toss my phone onto the counter and shake my head. Pulling open the freezer, I grab the bottle of tequila and pour myself more than a shot. Probably well more than two.

Taking a hefty sip, which burns for a few seconds after I swallow, I slam the glass on the counter and scream, "Fuuuuuck!"

One night.

One fucking night is going to ruin my whole fucking life.

Aimlessly pacing the apartment, I mutter to myself at every jumbled thought running through my mind.

The sleaze.

That all of this is Nikki's fault.

I should've said no.

Edmund.

And how he said nothing.

Fists pounding on the apartment door startle me from my thoughts. Pausing to place my near-empty glass on the counter, I make my way toward the door, shouting, "I'm fucking coming."

When I pull open the door, I'm shocked to find Edmund on the other side. Surprised enough that I don't manage to slam the door in his face before he steps into the apartment.

"I told you, I'm fucking done...with whatever this fucking is or wh——"

My words are silenced as he grips my face firmly and shoves me into the wall next to the front door. I hit it with a thud, briefly causing me to see stars. Looming over me, he grits his words through his teeth. "I told you to watch your fucking mouth."

He kicks the door shut with such force that it rattles the wall behind me. The grip he has on my face is painful, forcing me to grind my teeth as tears well in my eyes. "And you aren't fucking done with me because I'm not fucking done with you."

My chest heaves as he stares down at me. I'm so angry. So fucking mad at him. I want to fight him. I want to shove him away.

But I also want...

As though he can read my mind, his lips crash brutally against mine, causing me to gasp. A gasp he utilizes to press his tongue into my mouth. He plunders my mouth as my hatred grows into need. Undeniable, animalistic need.

Clawing at the back of his shirt, I pull it over his head, forcing him to break our kiss for a moment. A moment too long. Pinning me back against the wall, he reclaims my mouth with more passionate need than before as he roughly palms both of my breasts. He squeezes them so blissfully hard that I whimper into his mouth, which only makes him more feral.

Pulling from my lips, he spins me around and shoves my face into the wall. He yanks my leggings down over my ass, leaving them around my thighs, before pinning both of my wrists to the wall above my head with one hand.

Edmund presses between my thighs and shoves the entirety of his length inside of me with a single, deep thrust as he growls against the back of my neck.

"Mine."

He keeps a slow pace, but his thrusts are hard and demanding. Each of them is so intense that he bottoms out inside me. He sucks the crook of my neck, painfully hard, as he leaves yet another mark on me. His lips flutter against the already sore skin, and he groans, "We both know this is my fucking cunt, little rose. Don't we?"

"Yes," I shriek as the head of his cock slams into my cervix.

He pulls out before quickly slamming back into me with the same depth. Repeating the motion, he repeatedly slams against my cervix like a fucking battering ram. Pain and pleasure radiate through me with each drive.

"I'm. Going. To. Ensure. You. Don't. Fucking. Forget." He grunts each word against the back of my neck between thrusts, each more brutal than the last.

"Ed..." I begin to scream out his name, and my breath catches when he drives into me again, "...die."

"Again," he demands as he picks up his pace and lessens his depth. His words are breathless and heady when he commands, "Scream my name. Let everyone know whose fucking cunt this is. Scream it as I fucking fill you with my cum."

Hardly able to breathe as he continues to slam against my ass, I have no choice but to give him what he wants. The orgasm building at my center shoots through my body like fire. "It's yours, Eddie," I pant as I struggle to catch my breath through the painful euphoria.

"Mine," he roars as he slams into me. His cock twitches inside of me as his hips tremble against my ass. Filling me and marking me as his.

Continuing to pin me to the wall with his hands, and with his cock still deep in me, he presses his sweaty forehead to the nape of my neck. His deep, warm breaths blow against my back as he catches his breath. After taking a deep inhale, he whispers, "I'll fix this."

You have to...

CHAPTER TWENTY-TWO

EDMUND

> **Harper**
> I don't think I can do this.

> You can.

> But you don't have to.

> That video will ruin my life.

> Nikki's. Yours.

> Do NOT do this for me.

> I'd play the video of me taking your ass in the middle of Times Square.

> If you do this, you do it for you.

> I'm working on making this all go away.

Liz will lose her shit, but I've enlisted Grant to try to hack into Detective Asshole's devices to wipe the video in question from existence. He's doing it under the guise of me not wanting to tarnish my real estate empire, but he's doing it.

> It's just sex.

> It's never JUST sex.

> There are always feelings.

> Just these ones are disgust and disdain.

Anger, hatred, and rage are more accurate. Coupled with constant thoughts of putting his body beneath one of my builds.

The need to protect her—*protect what is mine*—and keep his hands away from her has consumed my mind since I walked out of her apartment the other day. Planning full and well to make good on my promise to her. Enough so that when the opportunity to run him down on Main Street presented itself, I floored the accelerator and nearly took him out. Broad daylight and too many witnesses are the only reason he's still vertical today.

> Open the door.

> What?

> Don't make me repeat myself, Harper.

> You know what happens when you don't listen.

She is at the door a moment later dressed in frumpy sweatpants, but her makeup and hair are fully done. She's looking as beautiful as ever.

Too fucking beautiful for him.

Grabbing Harper's wrist, I drag her through the main living area and down the hall to her bedroom. Pulling her inside, I shut the door, grip her throat, and tip her face up to mine.

"You don't have to do this." I place a rough kiss on her lips. "But you can. Nothing changes."

*I don't even know what **this** is.*

Slipping my hand into her pants, I cup her bare cunt. "This is mine, little rose. I'm not done with you yet."

Nearly a week of her—spilling myself inside of her at least once daily—and I still can't fucking get enough of her.

"You do what you *need* to do." I pull my hand from the front of her sweats before kissing her hard and deep.

If she is doing this, she's going to do it with the taste of me on her tongue.

"But if you tell me to make him go away, I'll happily oblige. And you'll never see him again."

Neither will anyone else.

"I'm good," she mumbles against my lips.

"If you change your mind—"

"I know," she interrupts me. "You'll be my first call."

Walking away from her, I hate the position that she's in. If we'd have just fucking killed him, this wouldn't be happening. But I know Will is right about the heat that will bring on all of us. Heat that will lead us all straight to the death chamber.

Opening the door, I nearly bump into Detective Asshole on my way out. "Hmph, Detective Michales. Funny running into you here. Are you related to Nikki?"

"Um, yeah," he lies, assuming he isn't blackmailing his niece to fuck her.

"I'd love to catch up," I spread a fake grin across my face, "but I need to get back to Adelaide Cove."

Where I'm going to figure out how to put your ass in the ground.

CHAPTER TWENTY-THREE

HARPER

Taking a seat on the couch by Nikki, I squeeze her hand as we both catch fragments of the interaction happening in the hallway between Eddie and the detective.

With the door left open, Michales lets himself inside. The face he makes upon seeing the two of us on the couch is strange, but I can't quite place it.

Disappointment?

He shuts the door behind himself and locks it before storming across the room. Standing over us, he is clearly angry when he asks, "What the fuck was Edmund Parker doing here?"

"He stopped by asking to see me again," I lie.

"And what did you say?" He tips his head with the same inquisitiveness as a dog.

"I told him I'd have to think about it," I lie again, hoping he can't tell.

"Did you fuck him?" His accusation is laced with envious jealousy.

"No." I shake my head, preparing to deceive him again. "I mean, yes. But only that night on the video."

He berates us with questions about Eddie and the party as though interrogating us. He's fixated on them, needing to know every tiny detail we're able to provide him with.

It was a consensual party.

It doesn't make any sense.

Out of nowhere, he firmly grips my face and pulls me from the couch. While forcing me to look at him, he demands, "You're going to say yes to him. Eagerly yes to everything he asks of you. And every week when I come by, you're going to tell me everything you've learned about him and the fucking rich assholes he associates with."

I don't have a response to him. I simply stare at him, trying to understand his fascination with Eddie and his friends.

"The more useful information you provide," he firmly grips my shoulder and viciously pushes me to my knees before him, "the less payment I'll require to keep your sweet, old nana from finding out what a dirty fucking whore you are."

Swallowing hard and gagging back the bile rising in my throat, I unzip his pants and pull out his flaccid dick.

I just want to get this over with it.

I place him in my mouth and take all of him in with ease. Hollowing my cheeks, I suck hard as I rub my tongue along the underside of his sweaty shaft, hoping he comes as quickly as he did for Nikki.

"You too," I hear him summon Nikki, and she promptly joins me on the floor. We both suck his cock, making a show for him as we both try to work him over the edge. He grows more rigid in my mouth, and I brace for him to fill it with cum. Instead, he loudly demands, "Enough."

He takes a step away from us, kicking off his shoes and removing his shirt. Pushing his pants down his thighs, he kicks them off and takes a seat in the chair beside our couch. Once comfortable, he begins leisurely fisting himself.

Never sitting there again...

"Clothes off," he commands. Standing before him, Nikki and I both discard our clothes and toss them onto the couch. Her hand brushes against mine, and she gives me a subtle nod before walking toward him.

She's going to take this bullet for us both.

"We have plenty of time." He waves her off, and his words hit me like a fist to the gut. "You're going to fuck each other first."

Walking back to me, Nikki mouths the words 'I'm sorry.'

"On the coffee table, Nikki." He points at the table, and she promptly does as he directs. "Spread your legs nice and wide for me, so I can watch Harper eat your cunt."

I can do this.

I've done this before.

Kneeling on the floor, I give her thigh a gentle squeeze and close my eyes. I do as he tells me and lick and suck her while pretending he isn't sitting a little over a foot behind me. His fingers twirl in my hair, causing me to startle. But it's his knuckles running down my spine that gives me goosebumps and causes tears to well in my eyes. He leans uncomfortably close, grabs my hand, and groans, "Use your fingers, Harper. I want you to make her come. I want her nice and wet."

Fighting back the urge to vomit, I slip my fingers in her. Curling them vigorously and sucking hard at her clit, I need her to come sheerly in the hope that it will remove his hand from me. Relief washes over me when she does, and his hand disappears.

"Good girls," he praises us. "Now, switch."

Swapping places, Nikki's face is immediately between my thighs. As much as I wanted to move away from the detective, this is worse. From here, I can see every repulsive face he makes as he watches.

My eyes are glued to him as he stands from his seat. Bending over, he pulls something from his pants before standing. He places the foil packet between his teeth and tears it open, quickly rolling the condom he retrieves from it down his clammy cock.

"Ass up, Nikki." He drops a pillow to the floor by her feet and kneels on it. She lifts herself onto her knees and squeezes my outer thigh for support. Reaching down, I grip her hand.

We're in this together.

Once inside of her, he comes fast. First time, never been in a pussy, fast. He pulls out, removes the condom, ties it off, and drops it on the table beside my leg. He nonchalantly gathers his clothes strewn across the floor and takes his time getting dressed. After tying his shoes, he grabs the condom and shoves it into his pocket.

"Next time, Harper." He winks at me before heading to the door.

The second he's in the hall, I clammer from the table and run to the kitchen sink. The mere thought of him being inside of me causes me to expel the contents of my stomach.

"Harp—"

"It's fine." I wipe my mouth with the back of my hand while I rinse out the sink. Turning off the water, I rush straight to my bathroom, where I plan to scrub myself clean of him.

Instead, I send a quick text to Eddie.

> It's over.

> He didn't fuck me.

EDDIE
Are you okay?

> No.

> But it had to be done.

CHAPTER
TWENTY-FOUR

EDMUND

It didn't *have to be done.*

It never should've fucking come to this.

The kid was right, we should've just fucking killed him.

I never left Harper. I've been waiting in my car across the street, waiting for her call. Ready to drag Detective Asshole from her apartment. Straight to the nearest dumpster after bludgeoning his face beyond recognition.

Watching him walk from her building, with the smug look of satisfaction plastered across his face, only fuels my need to remove him permanently from her presence.

Making him no longer a nuisance in all our lives.

Without pulling from my spot, I watch him diligently as he makes his way down the street and toward the parking garage. I open my car door and climb from the car before crossing the street and following him.

The garage has shit security surveillance.

I can end him—here and now.

My phone buzzes in the front pocket of my pants, and I pull it out as I continue to trail behind the detective.

HARPER
Can you come back?

Please…

I need you.

Fuck.

Shoving my phone back into my pocket, I turn on my heel and quickly walk down the block to her apartment. At the door, I use the key I helped myself to and head inside. Clothes are strewn across the couch, and neither of the girls is to be seen.

Entering Harper's room, I know she's in the bathroom as her shower is running. I flip the lock on the door and discard my clothes as I walk across the room, leaving a haphazard trail behind me.

When I pull back the curtain, Harper is vigorously scrubbing her skin with tears streaming down her face. She startles briefly at the sight of me before quickly throwing herself into my body and sobbing against my chest.

"If you're expecting me to comfort you and tell you everything will be okay," I pull the curtain shut and walk us into the spray of water, "you made the wrong call. I am not that man."

Pulling back from me slightly, she looks up at me with sad, bloodshot eyes.

I stare down at her and shake my head as I repeat myself, "I'm not that man, little rose. You know I'm not."

Gripping her sodden hair, I yank her head back with enough force to cause her to wince as I growl, "But I can make you forget."

I don't wait for her to answer. Using my body, I pin her to the shower wall. She hisses as her back arches from the icy tiles, sliding her already taut nipples over my skin. I press my knee between her thighs, forcing her to spread her legs for me.

"That's it," I praise her while dragging both of her hands up the tile and pushing them over her head. "Open those legs nice and fucking wide for me. Let me see what's mine."

Holding her hands firmly against the wall, I take a small step back, leaving a little space between us. Without warning, I bring my hand across her face with just enough force to sting. She's still startled when I forcefully grip her face and plunder my tongue in her mouth. Not releasing my grip, I pull back and gravelly whisper, "This is mine."

Sliding my hand down her jaw and along her throat, I tighten my fingers for a minute before continuing to trail along her collarbone and over the swell of her breast. I pinch her nipple, squeezing until she whimpers from the pain. Her cries only make me pull harder. I suck the other into my mouth and teasingly lick at it with my tongue— pleasing one and inflicting brutal pain on the other— leaving her a fucking mess in my hands.

I drag my teeth pleasingly over her nipple as I continue to torturously roll the other between the tight grip of my fingers. I sink my teeth into the meaty flesh of her breast, not stopping until she's pleading for me to stop, and there is a faint metallic taste on my tongue. Licking the blood oozing from my mark, I snarl, "Mine."

Releasing the bruising nipple between my fingers, I suck it into my mouth and gently caress it with my tongue until she's mewling from the pleasure on her tight, overstimulated bud of nerves.

I lift my head and stand over her, and she stares up at me with lust-filled eyes. Leaning down until our faces are only a hair apart, I slap my palm hard against her cunt. Her gasp blows across my face as I strike her clit again. "Mine."

I plunge two fingers inside her soaked channel, thrusting and curling them at a pace that will force her to come all over my hand. The hands above her head tug at my firm hold, and her thighs tremble against me. "Who owns this tight little cunt?"

"You," she pants, mere thrusts from losing herself. Thrusts I demandingly give her until screams are rushing over her lips, and she's quivering around my fingers. Slipping my cock along my palm, I press it deep inside her, replacing my fingers.

"You're going to need to tell me again, little rose," I release her hands, grip her thighs, and pull her legs around my waist. I fuck her hard and fast, giving her what she needs.

What we both fucking need.

Her near-breathless grunts blow against my shoulder and lips as I take her at such a savage pace that I know that I can't last. I clench my hand around her jaw and grunt against her lips. "Is this my fucking cunt?"

"Y...yes," she exhales.

"Do you want to be filled with my cum until I'm fucking dripping from you?" I breathlessly groan into her mouth.

"Please," she begs.

"Then fucking come for me." I slap her face, and she explodes. Her cunt clenches around me like a fucking a vise, squeezing me tightly as I continue to drive into her.

"FUCK!" I roar as I come, slamming my fist into the tile beside her face with such force it shatters. Relentlessly, I spill inside of her, emptying myself and filling her as I reclaim her as mine. I turn off the water and pull myself from her, watching my cum trickle down her thigh as I wrap her in a towel.

"Thank you." She stands on unsteady legs and awkwardly gives me her gratitude. I know it's not for the fuck but for clearing her mind, yet I can't help but smirk.

I've never had a woman actually thank me after fucking them before.

"Don't thank me yet, little rose." I pull her from the shower and drag her to the bed. "I have every intention of filling your other holes and marking your ass before I'm done with you tonight."

CHAPTER
TWENTY-FIVE

HARPER

The sun peeking through the window curtains wakes me. Rolling over, I find the bed empty, Eddie having slipped out at some point while I was asleep. He stayed with me in Vegas—not that he had anywhere else to go—but since then, he has repeatedly disappeared in the middle of the night.

I try not to let it bother me, but it stands as a steady reminder of what this is.

A fling.

Nothing more than a dark, dirty fling.

Too bad I know I'm fucking kidding myself. You don't fall for men like him. A man you've hardly known a week. A man you know you barely know anything about. A man who never takes you to his place. A walking red flag who always slinks out before sunrise.

There are always fucking feelings.

Being with him is like watching two trains on a collision course. It's going to end violently and messy, and someone is going to get hurt.

I'm going to get hurt.

I know it.

I can see it coming.

The opportunity to hop off this ride is there. I can take it at any time.

But fuck...this ride is fun.

Rolling over to grab my phone from the nightstand, I can't stifle my groan. Every fucking muscle in my body is sore. Muscles I didn't even know I had.

> You could really give a girl a complex...

> Sneaking out before sunrise every time.

> **EDDIE**
> I had somewhere to be this morning, little rose.

> I can barely move this morning.

> You really did a number on me.

> You needed it.

> Heading into a meeting.

> I'll text you later.

> K.

Sliding from bed, I pause to try to stretch my burning limbs. It does nothing for me except cause every inch of me to ache. Heading into the bathroom to pee, I catch a glimpse of myself in the mirror.

"This can't be healthy," I mutter to myself.

While Eddie might have left in the night, he's left several lasting reminders that he was here. Hickeys on my shoulders, scabbing bite marks on my breasts, and a permanently hard, very bruised nipple. Turning, I find my ass still red from the repeated, punishing strikes of his palm.

———

It's been hours since Eddie's text, and I haven't heard a thing from him. With my phone in my hand, I feel like I'm about to put myself into the needy girlfriend category, but I send the text anyway.

> Am I going to see you tonight?

> **EDDIE**
> At this rate, you might never sit again, little rose.

> But not tonight. I have a party to attend.

> What kind of party?

> A very private one.

With the text equivalent of word vomiting, the letters spill from my fingers, and I hit send before I can stop myself.

> The kind I met you at?

Yes.

Jealousy pangs through me. My face heats with anger yet tears well in my eyes.

Are you planning to fuck anyone there?

That is kind of the point of the party.

Seriously?

So my cunt belongs to you, but you can do whatever the fuck you want with your cock?

Don't feign innocence like you didn't suck someone else's cock yesterday?

Or have your face buried in your roommate's pussy.

That's not the same.

And you fucking know it.

I don't have time for this childishness right now, Harper.

Unable to hold them back, tears stream down my face as I continue to text him.

Apparently, the train was colliding sooner than I thought...

My apologies.

I wouldn't want to keep you from fucking someone else.

I'm not doing this with you.

It's just fucking sex.

It doesn't fucking matter.

It does.

It matters.

I'll call you in the morning.

When you've calmed down and are ready to
have an adult conversation about this.

I'm sorry I'm such a child.

Maybe you shouldn't bother.

I don't mean the words as I send them. Not even close. They couldn't be further from my truth. Staring at the phone through my sobs, I wait desperately for a response from him.

One that doesn't come.

CHAPTER TWENTY-SIX

EDMUND

Tossing my phone onto the bed, I run my fingers through my hair in frustration as I let out a deep, heavy sigh.

It's just fucking sex.

I've had my cock in countless—*meaningless*—cunts. That's all the one tonight is going to be. A woman who's nothing more than a set of fucking holes for my cock. Entirely willing to be used as I see fit.

Harper may fill that need for me too, but she can't seriously expect me to only dip my cock in her for the rest of my life.

Just her.

Forever.

Stepping into the party, Harper has tainted my whole fucking evening with her inadvertent demand for monogamy. The word is so foreign to me that it might as well be blasphemous.

"What's wrong, Eddie?" Liz saunters over to me when I enter the room. I've always hated the way that name sounded rolling off her tongue.

Unlike Harper.

I fucking love how she screams it for me.

"I hate when you call me that. I'm having a shitty evening and am not in the mood," I grumble, not wanting to elaborate on the truth.

What the fuck is the truth?

Why the fuck does Harper have me so aggravated?

"I guess it's a good thing that you've got a tight little ass waiting down the hall for you. You can fuck your frustration out on her," Liz smirks. Lifting her hand to my face, she drags it through my short beard, "Unless you want to take it out on me."

My hand snaps around her wrist, quickly yanking her from me. She gasps loud enough to garner Will's attention, and I quickly release her. She rubs her wrist before taking a step back from me, "Jesus, Edmund. Your girl is down the hall."

Paying no attention to the murderous gaze Will is giving me, I leave the room and head toward my plaything for the night. Liz is probably right. I just need to relieve my frustration.

That must be it.

Based on the sounds I pass as I make my way down the hall, either Grant or Samuel is well into their activities for the evening. Walking into the last room on the left, I'm met with tonight's leftovers—*brunette, pretty, fuckable*—spread eagle on the bed, offering up her cunt to me.

A cunt I've never found myself less interested in.

"Do you think you get to be a fucking pillow princess?" I huff, already loathing her as my girl for the evening. She takes her time leisurely crossing the room to me in a poor attempt to be seductive.

When she reaches me, I place my hand on her shoulder and shove her forcefully to the floor. Her knees hit the hard-wood floor with a thud, and the agonizing pain is immediately written across her face.

"You aren't here to be pleased." I undo my belt buckle, unbutton my pants, and lower my zipper. Freeing my cock with one hand, I use the other to pull my belt from my pants. "You're here to fucking please."

Firmly gripping the hair at the back of her head, I force my cock down her throat as she gags around me until her lips are circling the base of my shaft. Tears stream down her cheeks as I fuck her face significantly harder than she's used to.

This isn't doing shit for my disposition.

Swinging my arm, I crack my belt over her back, and she nearly cripples to the floor. My tight fistful of hair probably the only thing keeping her upright. I swing again, and she wails around my cock.

"A twenty-dollar whore sucks better fucking cock than you." I pull myself from her mouth.

"I can do it." She pushes the words out between sobs. Wrapping both hands around my cock, she fists over my shaft while sucking on my tip. Never taking more than an inch or two into her mouth.

No enthusiasm.

Nothing like my little rose.

"Sweetheart," I push her from me, "I don't know who told you were good at sucking cock, but they fucking lied to you. If you can't fucking swallow it, don't fucking bother."

"I'm sorr—"

"You should be." Fervently fisting my cock inches from her face, I grumble, "I've paid a lot of fucking money to be getting myself off."

Closing my eyes, I try to think of anything other than the useless warm hole kneeling before me. Even when I try to push her from my mind, every thought as I slide my fist over my length is of fucking Harper.

Her lips around my cock, eagerly swallowing every inch of me as I fuck her face. Taking me over and over as I glide down her tender, thoroughly used throat. Letting me use her until I spill down her throat, then sucking at my cock to get every last drop of cum from me.

My release shoots from my cock, splattering over the face before me. Tucking my cock back into my pants, I shake my head as it drips down her cheeks and over her lips.

"At least now you look like you fucking tried."

CHAPTER
TWENTY-SEVEN

HARPER

The bedroom door clicking shut startles me from my sleep. Glancing at the nightstand, I momentarily struggle to read the time on the alarm clock.

2:42 a.m.

I must've been fucking dreaming.

Rolling over and finding a comfortable spot in my pillow, my entire body grows rigid when the mattress shifts beneath me. I open my mouth to scream for help, but I can't. I'm so fucking terrified that not a sound comes from me.

"It's just me, little rose," Eddie slurs as his liquor-scented breath wafts over my face.

"It's almost three in the morning, Eddie." I shove him away from me.

"You wanted to see me tonight."

"No." I reach for the night table and flip on the blinding bedside lamp. Rolling back at him, I unleash all the feelings that caused me to cry myself to sleep only a few hours ago. My heart pounds with anger, tears well in my eyes again, and I shout, "I wanted to see you before you went to a party and fucked someone else. The absolute *last* thing I want is for you to climb in my bed *after* fucking someone else."

"Little ros—" His words are cut short when, unable to control myself, my hand slaps across his face.

His eyes darken, and before I have a chance to react, he's on top of me and has me pinned to the bed. My arms are shoved beside my head, and he pushes his weight onto them as he repositions himself so that he is straddling my waist.

"It will serve you well to not do that again," he grits through his tightly clenched jaw. "Understood?"

I don't answer him. I can't. Because the moment he lets go of me, I fully intend to slap him again.

He fucking deserves it.

Eddie firmly grips my face with his free hand and leans over me. Staring down at me, his breaths are deep and slow. "I didn't come here to say sorry."

"I sure as fuck hope you didn't come here to fuck me," I snidely quip, not liking the look in his eyes when he doesn't respond.

He throws back the blankets covering my legs and forces his hand between my thighs. His hand rubs over my panty-covered pussy as he announces, "I had to come here tonight."

"Get off." I struggle futilely against his massive weight that's pinning me in place.

"I had to come because you need to know."

"Know what?" I spit, still trying to wriggle my way from his hold.

He continues to rub over my pussy, his fingers dusting along the edge of the fabric as he slowly makes his way into my panties. Slipping a finger inside, he asserts, "This is my cunt."

Fuck him.

Fuck him and his ability to know exactly how to touch me.

"It's mine, little rose," he repeats as he continues to curl his fingers inside of me. Slowly making me forget why I currently hate him.

He continues to work me; my heart racing, no longer from anger, but from the ache building at my core needing to be relieved.

"Edd...ie," I pant, both trying to get him to stop and pleading for more.

"All mine. This cunt belongs to me." His voice is deep and commanding as he releases the tight grip on my wrists. Grabbing my hand, he roughly pulls it toward him and presses my palm to the crotch of his pants. He wraps his hand over mine and slides me over his length. "This belongs to you."

"What?" I blurt when his words catch me off-guard.

"I didn't fuck her, Harper." He continues to expertly slide his fingers in and out of me. "She fucking appalled me. You fucking ruined her for me."

"*I* ruined her?" I exclaim as my hips involuntarily rock to meet Eddie's touch.

"Yes," He slides his hand under my chin, gripping it firmly and holding my face toward his. His gaze is unwavering as he stares down at me. As he rubs the pad of his thumb over my clit, and I know the ache at my core is a ticking time bomb seconds from explosion. "Because she wasn't you."

His words throw me over the edge, and everything spills over. The orgasm tears through my body, pulling all my emotions with it. My back arches from the bed, and I scream through it all as tears fall from my eyes.

"I'm still mad at you." My words are breathy and heated.

"Be mad." A smug smile tugs at the corner of his mouth as he stands from the bed and quickly sheds his clothes.

"You can be as mad as you fucking want." He climbs back into bed and pulls me on top of him. Holding me firmly in place with one of his strong arms, he slides himself inside me. Brutally hard, he grips my ass with both hands, working me over his length. "But you can be fucking mad. Fucking furious even. As you ride my fucking cock."

CHAPTER TWENTY-EIGHT

EDMUND

Our limbs are strewn haphazardly across the bed—and each other—both of us are exhausted and satiated as the sun begins to peek over the horizon.

My fingers dust along the lightly marred flesh of her outer thigh, repeatedly tracing an imaginary line from her knee to the slight dimple of her ass cheek next to the handprint I left behind.

"What the fuck have you done to me, little rose?" I pose the question more to myself than to her.

She was spot on in Vegas. I don't do this.

Ever.

I don't cuddle. I don't bother with pillow talk.

Fuck, I've never stayed in someone's bed long enough for my head to hit the pillow.

Yet here I am. Post-fuck. Sprawled across this gorgeous woman's bed with her limbs draped over me. Completely fucking satisfied and still unable to pull my hands from her.

"I'm not the man you want me to be." I continue to stroke along her skin.

"I know," she whispers lightly against my chest.

"I'm not good for you."

"I know." Her tone is soft and solemn.

"I will never be good for you," I grip her thigh when she lifts her head to find my gaze, "because there is no good in me."

With her elbow propped on my chest, her fingers trace along my jaw, playing with the short hair of my beard as she softly disagrees, "I don't believe that."

"You should." I brush my fingers through her hair and lay her head back on my chest.

She doesn't have the faintest idea who I actually am.

How could she?

I haven't let her.

"I'm not saying you're a saint," she leisurely runs her fingers along the ridges of my abs, "but there is some good in everyone. No matter how minuscule."

"Maybe you're right," I surmise, vaguely liking the idea that she sees something in me that I don't see myself.

"This. Right now," she takes a deep breath as she nuzzles herself firmly against my body, "this is good, Eddie."

Gripping her thigh and wrapping my arm around her, I pull her tightly to me as I silently place my lips against her forehead.

This will never be enough for her.

We both know it.

Even with the sun blaring through the window, she falls asleep on me. This is generally when I slip out the door. But not this morning. I can't bring myself to pull my hands away from her body.

I watch her sleep as her soft, feathery breaths blow across my chest. Her warmth and the sun basking over my body eventually cause me to drift off as well.

CHAPTER TWENTY-NINE

HARPER

A couple of weeks later...

Sliding my hand along him, I teasingly circle my tongue around his tip. My sole purpose nothing more than to over-stimulate him and force him to come sooner than he wants. I firmly drag the tip of my tongue along the underside of his shaft when I quickly take him into my mouth, causing him to groan as his cock twitches.

He's already so fucking close.

Hollowing my cheeks, I suck harder as I vigorously slide my lips from base to tip.

"Fuck that feels good," he groans as he grows harder in my mouth. Knowing he's on the verge of coming, I pull my mouth from him. I vigorously pump my fist around him for a few seconds, causing him to spill himself on my bare tits.

Better than my fucking mouth.

So much better than my fucking pussy.

Grabbing my shirt, I quickly wipe every trace of him from me as though his putrid spunk is going to burn my skin.

"You suck cock like your life fucking depends on it." The detective stares down at me as he shoves his spent dick back into his pants.

Sure...

More like I just need it to be over.

"Don't think I don't know what you're doing." He looks at my tits and the balled-up cum-stained shirt in my hand. Terrified that he knows, my whole body tenses as the hair on the back of my neck stands on end.

Knowing the detective wants information, Eddie has been providing me with things to tell him; what his plans are for the next few days and where he'll be. But the things that really interest him are the ones about our sex life. That Eddie likes to leave marks on me during sex—with his hands, mouth, and toys. How brutally rough he likes to fuck me.

Beyond the shock factor or the possible gratification he gets from listening, I can't fathom why he would be interested in what I've been sharing with him.

But it's working.

During our last two meetings, I didn't need to lay a hand on him. Tonight, he was less than impressed with the information I provided him.

Or he's simply a disgusting sleaze of a man.

He's not the type of man who has a chance with women like us. Outside of his abhorrent personality, there is nothing remotely remarkable about him. Being able to take advantage of us is a power trip for him. A power trip that gives him an opportunity that he otherwise wouldn't have.

"You think I don't know that sucked my soul through my cock so I couldn't fuck you?"

"I didn't," I sputter as I shake my head, lying to his face. "I thought—"

His tongue glides over his teeth and hungrily along his lower lip as he continues to tower over me. He drags his rough knuckles along my jaw and lower lip as he threatens, "I do enjoy your mouth, but we both know that eventually you're not going to deliver. And when you don't, I'm going to find out what that sweet little cunt between your thighs feels like."

Thoroughly enjoying his thoughts, he palms his grim dick. I've never been so thankful that he's not only a quickdraw but that he's a one-and-done kind of guy. There is zero chance of him sticking around for round two.

"Let Nikki know I'll be by tomorrow night to collect, and I'm expecting info or ass." A devilish smirk spreads across his face. "And I do mean ass."

Poor fucking Nikki.

Since the first night, she has been taking the brunt of him. That night, it was so I didn't have to. I think, in part, it was her way of apologizing for putting me in this position in the first place.

A position I would probably be much angrier about if it hadn't connected me with Eddie.

She doesn't have an Eddie or any type of in with his inner circle. Zero chance of ever being able to give the detective what he wants. Except being inside her.

It's already taking a toll on her. While she's been fucking sugar daddies for a couple of years now, compartmentalizing it isn't appearing to come as easily when it comes to the detective.

The moment he walks out of the apartment door, I lock the handle and slide the deadbolt across. For good measure, I also hook the chain lock before heading to my room to bleach my mouth and scrub my tits until they bleed.

As I wait for the shower to warm, my phone buzzes across the vanity. Lifting the phone, I'm not surprised to find it's a text from Eddie. He knew I had a meeting tonight.

EDDIE
Do I need to kill him yet, little rose?

No.

Eddie has commented more than a few times that the detective will never fuck me and live to tell the tale.

And there's a small part of me that believes him.

More happened tonight than I plan to tell him, but how important is a ninety-second blowjob anyway.

If it even lasted that long.

It's not an argument we need to have again. I'm not willing to ruin everyone's life over this video. I can tolerate this until Eddie finds us all a way out.

> I have a few more hours of work.

> I'll call when I'm on my way.

> I want to listen to you as you get my cunt all nice and wet for me.

CHAPTER
THIRTY

HARPER

A couple more weeks later...

"Are you seriously not going to tell me anything? Not even where we're going?" I press.

Eddie doesn't make a sound as he continues to drive down the winding, tree-lined road. The only acknowledgment I receive is a firm squeeze from the hand wrapped around my thigh.

We finally pull to a slow crawl as we turn toward a large iron gate. It bears a similarity to the one from the mansion I met him at, but I don't think it's the same one. As he creeps closer to it, it begins to open. As soon as there's enough room for his car to fit through the opening, he stomps on the accelerator and catapults us down a long, curved drive. The mansion we race toward is definitely not the one I've been to before.

"Is this...your place?" I'm so caught off-guard that I barely ask my question. We've been seeing each other for a little over a month now, but not once have I been here. We spend nearly every night at my place, in my bed.

Nights spent elsewhere have always been a hotel in some city he flew me to for the night or the weekend. When he told me to pack a small bag for tonight, I just assumed that was going to be the case tonight. Especially since he's been talking incessantly about a little Cuban restaurant in Miami that he wants to take me to.

But not once has he mentioned me coming to his home. Coming here was so taboo that had he not been sleeping at my place for the past few weeks, I probably would've started to think that he was hiding a wife and kids.

"Yes." He gives my thigh a gentle, playful slap before sliding his hand from me.

Rounding the car, he opens my door and takes my hand to help me from it. As I climb out, a well-dressed older man descends the front steps of the house and walks toward us. Eddie hands him the keys to the car and instructs, "There's a bag in the trunk; please ensure it makes its way to my room. And send all the staff home for the weekend."

All the staff?

"Yes, sir." He quickly nods in acknowledgment before making his way to the trunk.

"Are you going to hold me hostage here all weekend?" I tease as we make our way up the steps and through the front door. Taking a look around, I lift my hand to my face to ensure my jaw isn't actually on the floor. His home is picturesque—straight out of some luxury home magazine. Natural light floods the space, only accentuating the soaring vaulted ceilings. His décor is modern yet minimalist. Everything is rich brown leather and dark wood, but it feels so cozy and welcoming.

It feels...like Eddie.

Dark and rough.

Like home.

"And what if I do plan to keep you here? As my little beck-and-call pain slut?" he jests.

"I mean," I overtly roll my eyes, "I guess I can make do."

"You're a little extra feisty today." He grips my chin and places a kiss against my lips. "That's good because you're going to need it for what I have in store for you."

Fuck.

I gulp at his words as he grabs my hand and pulls me through the foyer and main living area of the house, "This way, little rose."

The kitchen. So not the room I was expecting. Slipping his fingers from my hand, Eddie removes his suit jacket and carefully hangs it over the back of one of the island barstools. Dropping his cufflinks on the countertop, he meticulously rolls up each of his shirt sleeves, exposing his deliciously defined forearms.

Without saying a word, he opens the refrigerator and pulls several items out before walking around me to place them all on the counter beside the sink.

He fucking cooks?

Pushing past me again, he reaches into a cabinet, pulls out several pans, and sets each of them on the burners of the stove. He turns to face me, and I immediately realize that I am in his way again.

"I'll just go sit over there." I gesture at the stools on the far side of the island where he hung his coat.

"The fuck you will." He grips my waist and hoists me onto the counter. His hands roam over my hips and teasingly down my thighs. Reaching my knees, he grips them firmly and forcefully parts them. An uncontainable gasp escapes me, causing the corner of his mouth to tick up in a smile. His eyes never leave mine as he kneels before me and nips at my inner thigh just above my knee.

"Not yet, little rose." Eddie smirks before he rises to his feet with a cutting board in his hands. Laying it on the counter between me and the sink, he washes his hands, the scallops, and the produce he set out moments ago. He chops and dices the garlic, herbs, and tomatoes with finesse and precision. So skilled with a knife, one would think he's a professional chef, not a real estate tycoon.

After washing his hands and cleaning what little mess he's made, he leaves me for a moment. When he returns, he has a bottle of wine and two glasses in his hands. He pours a glass and extends it toward me. Stopping before I can take it from him, he raises a brow and questions, "Did you drink your water?"

"All sixty-four ounces of it," I smugly reply.

"Good girl." The deep tone of his praise travels straight to my pussy as he hands me the glass. "Because you're going to need it."

Oh fuck...

EDMUND

Pouring a glass of wine for myself, I place it and the bottle beside the stove. I click on each of the gas burners I need and move all my ingredients to the counter beside my wine.

"This just won't do." I part Harper's knees and step between them. Gripping her thighs, I pull her around my waist as she quickly wraps her arms around my neck when I begin to lift her.

Fuck, I love the feel of her wrapped around me.

Spinning around, I place her on the counter near the stove so I can still see her gorgeous face while I cook.

For her...

The enjoyment and comfort I get from cooking the perfect meal have always been just for me. Never in my life have cooked a meal for a woman. Not even my own belated mother. My love of cooking is a secret that no one has been privy to—before Harper. Yet here I am, sautéing garlic and tomatoes as I prepare to feed her my favorite meal.

"You continue to surprise me, Edmund Parker." She smiles over her wine glass.

I continue to surprise myself since meeting you...

Dipping a spoon into the creamy sauce, I blow on it before taking a small taste. After ensuring it's to my exacting standards, I slip the spoon between Harper's lips. She moans with delight as her lips wrap around the spoon, gathering every drop into her mouth.

"Oh my God, Eddie. Is there anything you don't do well?" she exclaims with a hint of sarcasm and flirtatiousness that causes me to smile back at her.

Keeping the women in my life alive.

I keep that thought to myself as I turn the stove burners off. I grab plates from the cabinet above me and serve each of us a helping of the Tuscan Butter Scallops.

Stepping in front of her, I wrap one hand around her waist and the other around her throat. I squeeze lightly and firmly press my lips against hers before pulling back and leaving her wanting more.

Leaving us both wanting more.

My lips still brushing hers, I speak against them as I lift her from the counter, "I was thinking we could eat outside by the pool. First, dinner. Then, you."

I slide her down my body until her toes touch the floor as a rosy blush creeps over her cheeks. I can't get enough of the way she reacts to me—to all of me. Even as she finds her balance, I don't quite want to let her go and my hands linger against her for a moment longer than necessary.

Harper grabs our wine glasses as I grab our plates, and she follows me through the French doors at the back of the house. After setting the plates on the table, I pull out her seat and gesture for her to sit. As I take mine, she lifts a pair of leather cuffs from the table with an inquisitive look on her face.

"Those are for dessert, little rose." I pull them from her hand and lay them back on the table between us with the other pair.

Harper enjoys bite after bite of the meal I prepared for her, savoring every mouthful as though she were trying it for the first time. The same way she seems to enjoy everything with me.

"You've really outdone yourself, Eddie." She forks another scallop and swipes it through the cream sauce on her plate. "This might be the most amazing thing I've ever eaten in my life."

"I used to be able to say the same," I finish off the final bit on my plate before continuing, "but that was before I had the pleasure of feasting on your delicious cunt."

That adorable crimson flushes her cheeks again, comparable in color to the shade I intend to make her ass shortly.

"Finish your wine," I rise from my seat and grab her plate, "while I run these inside."

When I return a moment later, she's standing poolside, sipping on the remainder of the Sauvignon Blanc. Stepping behind her, I snake my arm around her waist as I sweep her hair to the side.

"Are you ready to play, little rose?" I place a trail of rough, wet kisses from the crook of her neck up to her ear. Pressing my lips to the shell of her ear, I whisper, "Because I've been thinking of things I plan to do to you all fucking day."

Reaching her free hand up, she slides it through my hair. When she gets to the back of my neck, she pulls me into her, silently demanding more from me.

More, which I will gladly give her.

Grabbing her wine glass, I hastily toss it into the pool before us, and I pull her tighter to me. I slide my hand up her body and wrap it around her throat. Angling her chin up, I stretch her neck and grant myself unfettered access to her. I continue to kiss and nip before sucking hard. She groans as I leave my first mark of the evening.

"Your sweet sounds are delightful, little rose," I kiss over the bruising flesh on her neck, "but it's your pained cries and screams of absolute fucking pleasure that I'm looking forward to most of all."

CHAPTER THIRTY-TWO

HARPER

Edmund sinks his teeth into my shoulder, the pain shooting straight to my pussy and causing my knees to buckle beneath me. Kissing over the teeth marks I know he left behind, he gathers my tank top in his hands and swiftly pulls it over my head.

With his arms still wrapped around my waist and throat, he continues to kiss and bite my neck as he walks me across the patio and back to the table where we ate dinner. He doesn't stop until my hips are flush against the edge of it. Using his weight, he leans us both forward until my nipples are pressed against the cool glass of the table beneath me.

Grabbing a pair of the cuffs, he holds them as his knuckles dust down the length of my arm. The tingle of his soft touch causes my heart to race in anticipation. Reaching my wrist, he wraps the leather around me and secures the buckle. Placing my hand on the table, leaving the second cuff free, he slides his hand over my body as he makes his way around the table to where my other hand waits.

Lifting it, he places a soft, wet kiss against my palm as he skillfully fastens the second cuff around my wrist. Pulling my hand over the edge of the table as he kneels, he silently hooks the free cuff around the top of the table leg. My gaze follows his as he rounds the table, where he kisses my knuckles before securing the other cuff.

My chest heaves in anticipation—and a smidge of fear—as he steps back to admire the position he has me in. On my tiptoes, with the rough concrete digging into my toes, I'm bent at the waist with my upper body stretched across the table. With the width of the table, coupled with the cuffs holding me in place, I'm barely able to move.

Rounding the table, he steps behind me and presses his hand between my hips and the table to undo the button and zipper of my shorts. Gripping them at my hips, he drags them and my panties down my legs as he places soft kisses over the cheeks of my ass.

"Your panties are already soaked." His deep voice comes from behind me. "Are you excited, little rose?"

"Yes," I breathlessly whisper as he widens my stance.

"Nervous?"

"A little," I stammer.

"Good," he groans against my pussy before licking and sucking at me with enthusiasm. Moans and whimpers spew over my lips as his tongue masterfully swirls around my clit, knowing exactly how to bring me to the brink.

And that's as far as he brings me. Firmly licking through my pussy and up my ass, he stands behind me. He walks around the table, his fingers teasingly gliding over each inch of my body as he taunts me, "Sorry, little rose. Not yet. Not until your ass is red and that sweet cunt of yours is dripping down your thighs."

Standing where I can see him, he takes his time unrolling the sleeves of his shirt and undoing each button before removing it. He undoes his belt buckle and pulls it from his pants in a single, swift motion. "I want you a begging, fucking mess when you come all over me."

Folding over the leather of his belt, he wraps his fist around the buckle and the loose end. He returns to me and both the fold of the leather and his soft fingertips brush over my skin. My heavy breaths blow against the glass as I writhe in need against the table. Eddie lightly swats the leather against my ass, and I can't stifle the moan that rattles from me as it bites against my skin.

"More?" he continues to tease me.

"Yes," I exhale.

"Such a dirty little pain slut for me." He cracks the leather against my skin hard enough that I yelp. Pain and need flow through me, only growing when he strikes me again.

He slips his fingers into me and languidly curls and thrusts them. Every touch feels so fucking good that it takes no time for my release to begin building at my core. A release he doesn't give me as he slowly pulls his fingers from me.

Eddie continues to teasingly glide his fingers and the belt over every inch of my body——*every inch but where I need him* —as he edges me repeatedly.

Denying me yet again, he slaps the leather against the back of my thighs with enough force that my knees buckle when my legs quiver.

"Please," I plead as he strips from his pants. It feels like it's been hours, and my clit throbs as though he has denied me thousands of times.

"Is this what you want?" He leisurely fists himself. "Do you want to feel my hips slamming against that bright crimson ass of yours?"

Continuing to work his fist over his length, he bends over the table and grips my face. Pressing his lips to mine, he slips his tongue into my mouth and kisses me deeply. His tongue wrestles with mine until I'm breathless and moaning.

"My hips slamming against your tender cheeks as I fuck your soaked and dripping cunt?"

"Yes," I pant through both need and exhaustion.

"I'm going to need to hear you beg, little rose." Eddie walks behind me and settles himself between my feet. He tortuously rubs his tip along my pussy as he demands, "Tell me you need my fucking cock."

"Please," I beg as he drags it over my clit. "I need your cock inside of me."

His deep, gravelly tone nearly does me in.

"Such a good fucking girl."

CHAPTER THIRTY-THREE

EDMUND

Toying with her and denying her for over an hour, I need to be inside of her as much as she needs me there. Bruisingly gripping her hips, I sink myself in to the hilt in a single thrust. The feral sound that blows from her lips when I bottom out inside of her is fucking music to my ears.

Forcing myself to stay motionless, I grit through my teeth, "Now, beg me to fuck your needy cunt."

"Please, Eddie." Her voice is full of pain as she begs.

"More," I demand as I bring my palm down on the tender flesh of her ass.

"Please. I need to come," she pleads with breathless, tortured words, "Please...fuck *your* needy cunt."

"Oh, fuck, little rose." I slide my hand up her spine and into her hair. Wrapping it around my fist, I yank her head from the table as I begin to drive into her. So needy from the denial, it only takes a minute of deep, hard thrusts for her to come undone.

"Oh. God. Eddie." The heavy words rattle from her as I continue punishingly fucking her through the wave of euphoria.

"Are you...praying...to me...little rose?" I grunt out the words between thrusts. Keeping my brutal pace, I quickly draw another release from her before slowing my thrusts. As much as I want—*no, need*—to come inside her, I'm not ready for this to end just yet.

"I won't be a merciful god." I tighten my hold on her locks, forcing her to wince as I painfully arch her back. "There will be no grace. You're going to come, making a fucking mess of my cock, until I've had enough of you."

Edging myself, I pull orgasm after orgasm from her until even I have lost count. I drag yet another painfully blissful release from her, watching as her hands fist the edges of the table aggressively. Her lips trembling when she whimpers, "I can't."

"Just one more," I groan, not stopping my brisk, deep strokes, knowing I'm only thrusts from my own undoing. Her cunt continues convulsing around my cock, and there is no stopping the inevitable. My balls constrict as I bury myself in her, momentarily losing my control as I spill into her.

Loosening my grip on her hair, I gently lay her against the glass. I lean over her and press my sweaty body against her fatigued one to undo the cuffs binding her to the table. Her breaths are still deep and heavy when I scoop her into my arms and lift her listless body into mine.

"You are so fucking incredible," I whisper against her fore-head while carrying her into the house and to my room. "The way you take me, it's like you were fucking made for me."

She's so fucking perfect, it's like I dreamed her into existence.

Pulling back the covers, I gingerly lay her on the bed and leave her for a moment to grab some arnica cream and a towel from my bathroom. I purchased a container for myself a week ago—it was only a matter of time before I couldn't stop myself from bringing her here. By the time I return to the bed, her eyes are closed. Knowing how fucking spent I am, I can only imagine the extent of her exhaustion.

Opening the jar, I rub it between my hands to warm it before spreading it across her bruising ass. My touch causes her to whimper in her sleep, and I surprise myself when I comfort her. "I know, little rose. Just a little more. You need it."

After wiping my hands on the towel, I climb into bed and pull her into me.

I still need to feel her against me.

Wrapping my arm around her, I brush the sweaty tendrils of hair from her face as she sleepily nuzzles into me. I stare down at her, watching her sleep as I continue to stroke along the hair I tucked behind her ear.

She's perfect.

Perfect for me.

There isn't a scenario in this universe that I can fathom what I did to deserve her. I cannot think of a single redeemable moment of goodness I've put into the world.

But she's mine...

Mine.

I don't care if I'm not good for her, even if it ruins her.

"You're mine, little rose," I mutter quietly against her fore-head. "Only mine. I'm not fucking sharing you anymore."

The shit with Michales ends now.

The only way he will ever lay another hand on her will be over my fucking dead body.

He will never get the opportunity to be inside of what belongs to me.

CHAPTER THIRTY-FOUR

DETECTIVE MICHALES

As though someone flicked a fucking light switch, this town has turned on its end.

No disappearances.

No women claiming—*and recanting*—their recent assaults. Physical or sexual.

The only crime that has happened recently is a fabricated mugging that nearly killed Samuel Millington.

The recounting of the event is so fucking unbelievable that even the most inexperienced law enforcement officer should be able to see straight through it. But they won't. Just like every other time these pretentious assholes wander before the law, the town will turn a blind eye and believe every inconceivable word that flows from their

My whole fucking life is in shambles because I'm the only one that sees it. It's time that changes. It's time for *their* lives to be the ones in shambles. The entire fucking town watching as their facades crumble, and everyone finally sees who they all really are.

Whatever it fucking takes...

CHAPTER THIRTY-FIVE

HARPER

> **Detective Sleazeball**
> You available?

> At work.

I type the lie and send it before stopping to think.

Fuck. What if he knows I don't have a job?

> Don't lie to me Harper.

> I'm not.

I lie again and decide to lean into it.

> You can call them.

> I don't get off until eleven.

> Just you.

> > Ok.

Eddie left several hours ago suddenly. Informing me that he didn't have time to explain, he gave me a kiss, a promise of a call, and strict instructions. Under no circumstances am I to leave his place or open the door *to anyone*.

I pace for a moment, knowing I need to go and meet the detective tonight, but also knowing that Eddie will be fucking livid if I do.

> > He wants to see me.

> **Eddie**
> No.

> > He's going to be at the apartment at midnight.

> And you aren't!

> > I just got to the hospital to check on my friend. I will be home within the hour.

> > So fucking help me if you leave before I get there.

My thumbs rest against the screen, trying to figure out my response, when another message from Eddie pops up.

> Do I need to get back in the fucking car? Or are you going to tell me you aren't going anywhere?

> > I'm staying put.

Good girl.

I set the phone down for a second before lifting it back off the table to text Nikki.

Call me.

I wait a few minutes before trying to call her. It goes straight to voicemail, and as usual, her inbox is full.

Do not go home tonight.

Stay anywhere else.

You can come here if you need to.

As promised, Eddie walks through the door within the hour. His arms are immediately wrapped around me, pulling me close—*possessively tight*—as he places a firm kiss against the top of my head.

"I told you." He pulls back and firmly cups my face between his hands. "He's never fucking putting so much as a hand on your again."

"But the video? Nikki?" I blurt out.

"Fuck the video," he continues to hold my face tightly. "And she's a big fucking girl; she can take care of herself. You will never fucking be alone with him again, understood?"

I nod, struggling against the vise that's keeping my face tilted toward his. Eddie stares down at me, his gaze dark. "You are mine. And he will not touch what is mine."

Tears well in my eyes, both from his painful grip on my face and his words.

His.

Not my cunt.

But me...

He's claiming me.

————————

Just after eleven, Eddie sends a text from my phone.

> Edmund picked me up.
>
> He isn't bringing me home.
>
> I can't get away.
>
> He'll be suspicious.

Detective Sleazeball
That wasn't the arrangement, Harper.

"Fuck the arrangement," Edmund seethes as he hands me back my phone. "He's lucky to still be breathing."

————————

Between one of his many trips to the hospital the last couple of days, Eddie went to my apartment and packed a large suitcase with more of my things because he was adamant that I was not leaving his place.

Not while there is the possibility of the detective coming to see me.

I've been dodging his texts and giving him the run around for days, blaming it on Eddie wanting me close since the mugging and near-death of his friend. While the detective isn't pleased, it's been working.

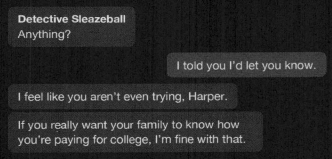

Detective Sleazeball
Anything?

I told you I'd let you know.

I feel like you aren't even trying, Harper.

If you really want your family to know how you're paying for college, I'm fine with that.

It's been days of threats. With every day that passes, I become even more disgusted with myself about the things I did to keep him silent because he's shown his hand. He's not going to share the video. He never had any fucking intention of actually exposing us.

He doesn't have the fucking balls to go through with it.

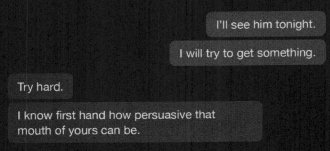

I'll see him tonight.

I will try to get something.

Try hard.

I know first hand how persuasive that mouth of yours can be.

I screenshot the exchange and send it to Eddie.

Eddie
He's not wrong...

Your mouth is pretty fucking persuasive.

But that cunt of yours could crumble fucking empires.

You sound better.

The kid is getting discharged.

I'll be home shortly, for a few hours.

All of which I plan to spend inside of you.

CHAPTER THIRTY-SIX

EDMUND

A few weeks later...

When everything happened with Samuel, I refused to allow Harper to leave my place for her own safety. In the past few weeks, though, I've grown used to her being here.

I like having her here.

In my home.

In my bed.

In my life.

At this point, I have no intention of letting her leave. However, it appears that she seems to be more than content with my stance on the situation.

The house is relatively quiet when I get home from work with the exception of the faint sound of music coming down the stairs. Following the melody, I find Harper in our bedroom, finding a place for a few more things from her apartment.

Oblivious to my arrival, she continues to dance, her hips swaying and gyrating to the sensual beat. Leaning a shoulder against the doorframe, I quietly watch her. Silently enjoying the small moment of absolute normalcy.

"Fuck! Eddie!" she shrieks when she spins around to find me staring at her, her ever-adorable blush creeping over her cheeks.

Removing my jacket, I toss it onto the settee at the end of the bed as I stalk toward her. Gently slipping my finger under her chin, I tip her face up toward mine as I shake my head.

"You have nothing to be embarrassed about, little rose." I grab her hand lightly, pull it between us, and over my rigid cock. "Absolutely nothing."

Gripping the bottom of her shirt, I pull it over her head and it slides over her pert tits. A light growl rises from me when her tight nipples slide from beneath the fabric. Continuing to stare into her deep blue pools, I unbutton her shorts, push them over her hips, and let them fall to the floor. I slip my fingers under the sheer panties and push them over her ass. They slide down her legs and into the shorts sitting around her ankles.

"On your knees," I command, and she willingly kneels for me, "Remove my pants. My shoes. My socks. Then show me how well you can suck my fucking cock."

Without hesitation, she follows each of my instructions. With my cock in her mouth, she slides her hands along the base of my shaft as she takes me deeper into her throat. Watching as she enthusiastically swallows my cock, I loosen my tie and unbutton my shirt. She swirls her tongue around my tip, and I moan as I slip out of my remaining clothes.

"Hands," I demand as I pull my tie over my head. Without missing a beat, she continues to bob over my length as she places her hands on my stomach. Slipping my tie around her wrists, I cinch it tightly as I praise, "That's my good fucking girl."

Lightly cupping her chin, I slide her off my cock before helping her to her feet. Using the tie like a leash, I lead her across the room to the bed and instruct her to get on it. When she settles against the pillows and the headboard, I grab the tie and pull her hands between her thighs.

"Show me how you fuck that perfect cunt of mine," I insist as I grab a bottle of lube from the nightstand and settle on my knees between her legs.

Harper slides her fingers through her arousal and rubs them in circles around her clit. Her touch varies between teasing and firm, as her body quickly reacts. I squeeze a generous amount of lube into my hand and lightly fist myself to spread it over my cock as she wavers on the brink of coming undone.

"Do you need a little help?" I press two fingers into her slick cunt as I continue to run my other hand over my length. As I curl inside her, she vigorously rubs over her clit, demanding her orgasm. Her thighs flex, and she clenches around my fingers. A satisfied moan grumbles from her before she slows the thrumming of her clit, continuing to tease herself as she prolongs the moment of pleasure.

Grabbing the slack of the tie, I pull her hands to my face and press her fingers into my mouth to suck the sweet taste from them.

She always tastes so fucking good.

Slowly, I drag her fingers from my mouth and pull her hands over her head. With the tie in my hand, I grip the headboard with one hand as I use the other to press my cock against the tight hole of her ass.

"Later, I'll make that sweet ass of yours a beautiful cherry red," I push against her finding a little resistance, "but right now, I want to fucking be inside it."

Staring into her blue eyes, I press the tip of my well-lubed cock into her eager ass. She lets out a pained moan as I slowly stretch her out for me. I work myself gingerly in and out of her tight hole until I'm able to do so with ease. My lips on hers and her legs wrapped around my waist, and I take her with long, deep strokes until we are both floating in bliss.

Pulling myself from her, I continue to kiss over her lips and cheeks. She stares up at me with a look unlike another.

Her eyes are full of adoration. Warmth. Devotion.

Love.

She might have fallen for me, but somewhere, I've completely lost myself in her.

CHAPTER THIRTY-SEVEN

DETECTIVE MICHALES

Pacing along the back wall of my home office, my gaze wanders over the photos pinned to the wall.

Grant Geyer, Edmund Parker, Samuel Millington, William Cattaneo, Elizabeth Beaufort.

The new women with three of them—supposedly willingly—Abigail, Cora, and fucking Harper.

She hasn't spoken to me in several weeks. My number is either blocked in her phone or she is outright ignoring every message that I've sent her. Every last fucking one of them.

Her little whore of a roommate hasn't yet had quite the same balls, and for fear of being exposed, she's picked up Harper's slack. While I'm still thoroughly enjoying using all of her holes a few times a week, she is deeming herself to be utterly useless in comparison to Harper.

Tearing her photo from the wall, I hold it in my hands and stare at it. Heat rushes up my neck and over my face as I continue to try to find anything to catapult my case forward.

But there's nothing.

Harper provided me with weeks' worth of useless fucking information. Shit she isn't fucking smart enough to figure out on her own. Things he had to have been feeding her. Bullshit lies he knew I would be happy to receive and subsequently waste my fucking time chasing after leads that weren't there.

The behavior of a guilty fucking man.

She's been playing me.

This whole fucking time. I pushed her toward him, needing her to get me information from the inside that I could never obtain otherwise, but she fucking willing ran into his arms. And together, the two of them have been playing me.

Laughing at me.

Fucking mocking me.

"You fucked me, Harper," I spit at the photo in my hand. My jaw is clenched painfully tight as I crumple the photo in my fist. Tossing it to the ground, I grit through my teeth, "You'll fucking pay for trying to deceive me."

Grabbing my keys from the table, I storm out the door to my pickup truck. Slamming the door shut as I climb in, I grumble to myself, "You'll pay. And when you do, Edmund Parker will show his fucking hand."

Slipping the truck into gear, I speed across town toward Edmund Parker's home. She'll have to leave eventually.

And I can be a patient man.

————

Hiding in plain sight for two days, my attention perks up when the gates open, and Edmund pulls through in his Bentley. It's the brand new, white Maserati following behind him that really piques my interest.

Did he buy her a fucking car?

Pulling from the shoulder and onto the road, I follow a few car lengths behind Harper. Through town and onto the interstate. Quite certain I know where we're heading, I'm not surprised to find us pulling into the parking garage around the corner from her apartment.

Following the Maserati up the levels, I continue past her when she pulls into a spot. I round the corner and quickly park.

I could take her right now.

The garage is devoid of people, and the security is shit. I could do what I need to do and be done with it. Ensuring to stay light on my feet so she doesn't hear me coming, I begin to close the distance between us. A few feet from the exit, I reach out to her. My hand lingers a hair from her shoulder, and a boisterous couple pushes through the door. She stops to talk to them, and I obscure my face as I briskly walk around her.

Your apartment it is.

Tucking myself into the alleyway between the garage and her apartment, I continue to wait. She walks past moments later. I almost follow straight behind her, but I opt to wait a few minutes.

Staring at my watch, I count the seconds until ten minutes have passed before stepping from the alley. I quickly walk into her building and disregard the requirement to stop at the security desk.

"Sir," the man behind the desk calls after me. "I can't let you up without signing in and verifying the residents are——"

"This is a police matter." I flash my badge at him. "Do you really want to impede a police investigation?"

"I'm sorry, sir." He quickly recoils and takes his seat as I step onto the elevator.

As I push the button for her floor, my heart begins to race as the doors close. Unable to stop myself, I send her a text.

> Time's up, Harper.

> I know you've been fucking lying to me this whole time.

> We're going to fucking talk.

> NOW.

CHAPTER THIRTY-EIGHT

EDMUND

"This has been a great pleasure, gentleman," I shake hands with the three white-haired men sitting across the board-room table from me as I continue, "I appreciate you taking the time and your gracious—and unanimous—agreement that expanding The Plantation will be a great addition to Adelaide Cove."

Gracious, my ass.

One hundred thousand dollars to each of those small-minded townies to agree to rezone the thirty acres of marshland abutting my current development. A bribe well-fueled by the sudden and untimely removal of Mr. Marshall from the zoning board. But thirty acres of prime real estate that I will more than make back my small investment on.

Walking from the boardroom, I pull my phone from my jacket pocket. It's been buzzing against my chest for the last ten minutes. Swiping the screen, I have six missed calls from Harper and nearly twice as many text messages.

"So needy," I chuckle to myself as I open the texts.

> **HARPER**
> He knows.

> Eddie, he's so angry.

> He's on his way.

> Please call me.

> What do I do?

> Eddie?

> I don't know what to do!

> Nikki isn't here.

> Why aren't you answering?

> Eddie?

> Please!

My stomach drops as I read them. My instincts told me not to let her go alone to grab more of things. The sinking feeling only grows when two more pop up on the screen.

> He's here.

> He won't stop banging on the door.

Before I realize it, I'm running toward my car as I dial her number.

"Eddie..." she trembles my name. *She's fucking terrified.* Two syllables, and there is no denying that she is absolutely petrified and on the verge of tears.

"Fuck! I'm on my way, little rose."

The sounds of his fists slamming against the door rattle the speakers of my car.

I'm never going to fucking get to her before he does.

"Get in Nikki's bedroom," I shout into the phone, listening to the wooden door slowly give way as I swerve between cars at reckless speeds. "It'll buy you a little time. And lock the fucking door!"

"Ed——" she cries.

"Just fucking do it," I shout over her, needing put space between them just a little while longer. But it's too fucking late. Harper's shrill screams and the door splintering from the frame flood the air in my car.

The screaming doesn't stop as I listen to him hit her over and over again. Loud crashes. Broken glass. Her screams grow quieter with every minute that passes, while the thumping of my heart only gets louder.

Her phone clatters against the hardwood floor, and she suddenly sounds galaxies away. Becoming further from me as I'm trying desperately to get to her.

"Please," she whimpers between sobs as more crashes and bangs continue to consume me. "No..."

"What's the matter?" Michales's angered voice oozes through the speakers. "I thought you liked it fucking rough."

"You're a fucking dead man!" I yell as my blood begins to boil and uncontrollable rage takes over. My grip on the steering wheel is so fucking tight that my knuckles are white, and my fingers ache.

It's nothing in comparison to the pain I feel with every hit I hear Harper endure. A deep, agonizing, indescribable pain. One that tears at my heart with every blow.

"I'm almost there, little rose." I veer off the highway as her screams and cries slowly subside until there is nothing but silence.

Absolutely terrifying silence.

Still minutes away, I scream my rage into the void until my lungs are empty. My whole body shakes as it builds again, violently demanding to be released.

Not a sound comes through the speakers.

Not Michales.

Not a single whimper or heavy breath from Harper.

Deathly painful silence.

CHAPTER THIRTY-NINE

EDMUND

Finally reaching her apartment building, I pull to a stop in the middle of the street and scramble from the car. When I get inside, I race toward the elevators and slap my hand against the call button incessantly.

Fuck, this is taking too long.

I barrel through the door into the stairwell and hurtle up the three flights of stairs. Pushing into her hallway, the door to her apartment is splintered in pieces and hangs off the hinges.

"Harper!" I scream as I step into the destroyed apartment. It looks like a fucking bomb went off. The floor is riddled with broken lamps, trinkets, and books from the overturned shelves. The glass crunches under my shoes as I continue to make my way inside, yelling her name again. "Harper!"

Rounding the kitchen island, my heart fucking stops when I see her. Her crumpled body lays among the broken plates and glasses covering the tile floor.

Bruised.

Bloody.

Fucking lifeless.

"Harper," I exhale her name as I drop to my knees beside her, barely registering the shards of glass piercing my skin. Swiping her blood-matted hair from her face, I slide my hand along her neck, desperately searching for a pulse. A faint heartbeat flutters against my finger, and I breathe for the first time since getting to her. Slipping my hands under her back and thighs, she groans when I scoop her off the ground. Glass clatters to the ground as I lift us both from the floor.

"I know, little rose. I know," I whisper as I pull her to my chest. "I've got you now."

Holding her tightly to me and trying not to jostle her broken body, I quickly get us downstairs to my abandoned car. Nudging the still ajar driver's side door with my elbow, I slide in with her on my lap. Her bloodied face rests against my chest as I shift the car into the drive and hurtle toward the hospital.

Racing through traffic, I steer with one hand as much as is possible. My other hand rests on her neck to feel her pulse fluttering against the other to know that she's still with me.

The light before us turns red, but I refuse to stop. Swerving through the oncoming traffic, I blow through the intersection. Harper moves slightly on my lap, wincing in pain.

"You're okay. I've got you," I try to comfort her, lightly running my fingers along the side of her neck as I use my grip to gently hold her to me.

Tears fall from between her lashes, trickling down her cheeks and to my hand.

"I know it hurts, little rose," I mutter against her forehead, wishing I could absorb her pain.

Pain, that is my fault.

"Just a little further," I continue to talk to her, even though I don't think she can hear me. "We're almost there."

"Ed..." Her eyelids flutter, revealing the broken blood vessels in her eye.

"Shhh." I breathe a sigh of relief that she's still fucking here with me.

"Eddie," she painfully pushes out my name.

"Save your strength."

"I love you..." she whispers the words as her heavy eyelids begin to close.

"No." I grit down at her as I pull her tighter to me than I should. "Don't you do that."

"I do." She lightly runs her fingers along my jaw as she continues to whisper breathlessly, "I love you."

"Don't you dare fucking say goodbye," I angrily growl at her.

Her fingers slide from my face, and her body is suddenly lax and heavy against me.

"You aren't fucking leaving me, Harper," I yell at her, begging her to hold on just a few minutes longer. "I'm not fucking done with you yet."

The final minutes to the hospital feel like an eternity. Squealing to a stop outside the emergency room, I wail on the horn for a second before sliding us both out of the car.

Her body is completely limp in my arms, her limbs dangling lifelessly beneath her.

I was too fucking late...

The sliding doors part, and I yell, "Help! I need fucking help!"

People in scrubs swarm us both, quickly putting Harper on a stretcher and whisking her away from me. As though suddenly crippled with an unbearable weight, I fall to my knees on the cold tile floor.

I never told her that I love her, too.

CHAPTER FORTY

EDMUND

Pacing the hallway, I try Samuel again. I need them all here because they need to know.

This is the end.

Voicemail, again.

"Pick up the phone, kid. It's Harper. Michales has gone too far. He's a fucking dead man."

"Sir," an older nurse approaches me , "We should really take care of you, too."

"I said I'm fucking fine," I seethe.

"With all due respect," she gestures to my legs and the faint bloody footprints I'm leaving along the corridor, "you aren't."

Begrudgingly, I follow behind her as she leads me to an exam room. Pulling shut the curtain, she directs me to th bed before cutting up the legs of my pants with a pair of shears. My legs are pocked with blood, small shards of glass protruding from my skin along the length of my shins to my knees.

"I'm fine," I repeat, "I can take care of this on my own."

"You're a stubborn fucker, aren't you?" She places her hand on my chest and shoves me back onto the bed. "You can't do anything for her right this minute. Just let me get you cleaned up."

"How is she?" I ask, having not heard anything since they swept her gurney down the hall over an hour ago.

"She's in surgery," she pulls out her phone and types across the screen, "but I'll see what I can find out for you."

"Thank you." I nod as she puts on a fresh pair of gloves. She meticulously plucks each piece of glass from my legs, dropping them into a small stainless-steel pan. "Are you supposed to talk to patients like that?"

"No." She removes a large shard that causes me to grit my teeth. "But I made an exception for you."

By the time Grant and Abigail arrive, the nurse has finished cleaning my wounds. Abigail is carrying a pair of my shoes and set of hangers, with a pair of my pants and one of my dress shirts. She puts them at the edge of the bed and asks, "Any word?"

"Nothing yet." I stand and strip from my ruined pants and blood-stained shirt. Stepping on the pedal for the biohazard container, the lid opens, and I drop everything into it. I grab my blood-sodden shoes and toss them in as well, wincing when I bend down. Lifting the new clothes from the bed, I quickly pull them on and got to find the nurse for an update on Harper.

Seeing me approach, she steps from behind the nurses' station. "She's still in surgery, but they are in the process of finishing up. She should be getting moved to recovery within the next thirty minutes."

The nurse leads the three of us toward a private waiting room so that we can have some privacy while I wait to see Harper. A disheveled Samuel and Cora join us shortly after we take seats. Their girls have quickly become part of our dysfunctional family, and the five of us call Will and Liz, who are currently on a short trip to Condado.

"He's gone too far this time." I speak over everyone.

"We're not arguing that." Liz's voice comes through the speakerphone. "He's still a fucking cop, Eddie."

"He's a dirty fucking cop who's been meddling in our lives for too long," I rebut. "But this isn't meddling anymore."

I turn my attention to Grant. "Would you stand by if he laid a hand on Abigail?"

Then, to Samuel. "Or Cora? No. He'd be fucking six feet under already."

"I'm not saying you can't," Grant replies, "because I know you're right. I'd probably have my hands around his throat by now. But this can't be rash."

"We have to be smart," Will chimes in. "It can't look like we killed him."

"That's your expertise, isn't it?" Inadvertently, I divulge Will's secret past to the group. "Fucking help me make it happen."

"We're pulling into the airfield now. We should be there in about four hours. I'll get a plan together during our flight. Get things in motion. It can happen tonight."

"He needs to pay, Will." I place my palms on the table flanked the phone. "Death isn't punishment enough. He needs to suffer for what he did to her. For trying to take her from me."

The things I plan to do to him...

Death will be a welcomed ending.

One he's fucking begging for.

"Understood," he replies before ending the call.

CHAPTER FORTY-ONE

EDMUND

Samuel and Cora left a bit ago to get cleaned up. Grant and Abigail are about to head home as well to work on a few items for tonight. As they leave, I glance down at my watch and realize that it's been nearly an hour since I spoke with the nurse.

Harper should be in recovery by now.

With me sitting by her side.

I'm about to go hunt down the nurse when she walks into the room with a solemn look on her face. Taking one look at her, I blurt out, "Is she dead?"

"No." She quickly grabs my hand. "She coded as they were closing her up."

Oh God...

"They were able to bring her back. But they had to go back in. I've been assured they're finishing up now. She'll be in recovery in about ten minutes. I can take you there now."

Following behind her, she leads me into a private suite to wait for Harper. No more than a few minutes later, she is wheeled through the doorway.

"Fuck, little rose," I gasp when I see her. Tubes and wires protrude from her bruised body. I grip her hand as she passes and walk with the bed until they have her settled in the middle of the room. Without releasing her hand, I pull a chair closer to sit beside her.

"We have her pretty heavily medicated," the doctor says from the other side of the bed. "She's going to be in a lot of pain, and we want to keep her comfortable overnight so that there is less stress on her heart."

I nod as I listen to him, just relieved to finally have her soft, warm hand in mine again.

"Stay. Talk to her." He closes her chart. "Just let her sleep, and know that if she does wake up tonight, she isn't going to be very lucid."

As he leaves us, he closes the door behind him.

I press my lips to the back of Harper's hand as I hold it in mine. With my lips vibrating against her skin, I vow, "He's going to regret ever meeting you, little rose. And he will never fucking touch you again."

Never letting go of her hand, I sit at her bedside for hours. The sun falls over the horizon as I kiss her knuckles and beg her for forgiveness.

Forgiveness she can't give me.

Just shy of midnight, Grant and Abigail step through the doorway into Harper's hospital room. With her dainty hand in mine, I rise from my seat and offer it to Abigail.

"I'm going to leave you with Abigail for a bit," I kiss the back of her hand before passing it over. "I have to go take care of something for you."

I lean over her bed until my face is inches from hers. Gently, I place a soft kiss beside the sutured gash on her forehead. Another on her well-bruised cheek. And one beside her ear as I whisper, "I love you, little rose. And I promise, this will be the last time I ever leave you."

Standing over the bed, I tenderly slide my finger along her jaw as I take a heavy breath.

"I'm ready." I turn toward Grant and ask, "Is everyone else?"

He gives a single nod, and the two of us walk from Harper's room. Silently, we make our way to the parking garage, where Will and Samuel are waiting in a blacked-out Suburban.

The four of us are in this together.

If one of us goes down, we all go down .

Crossing town, we make it to Detective Asshole's house in about twenty minutes. His meager home is nestled between trees on a desolate country road. His nearest neighbor is a mile away—too far away to hear his screams that are coming.

"We walk from here." Will pulls the SUV to the side of the road at the edge of Michales's driveway. "Unless he's a sound sleeper, there's no way the ground being churned up by the SUV won't wake him. I'll come back for the car when we're done."

Reaching the cabin, we all pull on a pair of gloves. There will be no evidence that any of us were ever here.

Will enters first, and the rest of us follow silently behind him. All of us stealthily make our way to the bedroom at the back of the house. Flanking the bed, Will grabs the pistol from the nightstand beside him as I flip on the small lamp on the one next to me.

"What the fuck!" Michales startles from his sleep to find me looming over him. Quickly rolling over to reach for his gun, he finds himself face-to-face with the barrel of it.

"I wouldn't." Will presses the muzzle to his forehead.

CHAPTER
FORTY-TWO

DETECTIVE MICHALES

Pushing back from the gun pressed to my face, I quickly realize that my room is full of the men I've been investigating.

Grant.

William.

Samuel.

And Edmund.

The four of them surrounding my bed. They are clearly not here with good intentions.

"Up." William gestures with the gun.

I climb from the bed, and they escort me to my office and turn on the light. Their eyes roam over the photos pinned to my wall as William shoves me into the seat behind my desk.

"You got this one wrong." Samuel taps his finger against a photo of a pretty brunette hung beneath the photo of him. *Kaylie*. "This one wasn't me."

"That one was Liz actually," William divulges. "She was less than pleased to come home to find my cock inside of someone without her."

"I thought she looked familiar," Edmund imparts before asking. "921 Ruby Ridge?"

William gives a nod, silently blowing my entire case wide open.

The girls.

The Preserves.

Every last one of them. They've been right in front of us this entire time. Slowly being buried beneath properties Edmund is constructing.

"All of you." I shake my head. "You're all the depraved pieces of shit I've been ranting about. Everything. You're all guilty as fucking sin."

"You aren't exactly innocent." Grant tosses a folder on the desk before me, photos spilling from it when it hits Michales' chest.

I lift the the small stack and rifle through it before exclaiming, "I don't know any of these women. Except—"

"You should," Grant interrupts. "You've been so entangled in our lives that I was quite disappointed to learn how many of our indiscretions you had missed when I came by earlier today. Shoddy fucking police work, if you want my opinion."

Dropping the photos onto the desk, I attempt to stand, pausing when William presses the gun to the back of my neck and shoves me back into my seat.

"But now," Samuel removes his photo from the wall and replaces it with two of the women from the desk, "they're your indiscretions."

"It will never stick!" I exclaim as he removes each of the men's photos from my wall. Taking his time, he slowly papers the wall with photos of gorgeous coeds.

"This town has been watching you spiral," Grant taunts me. "Losing your wife. Your kids. Even your job. All while trying to convince everyone that the *rich, upstanding men* of this town were responsible for the crimes you were committing."

"No one will ever fucking believe that!" I shake my head

"Who's going to tell them otherwise?" Edmund questions as Samuel presses a pin through a final photograph.

Harper.

"This wall is riddled with your fingerprints." Samuel shoves the pictures of each of them into his pocket. "And you mailed your confession to the Adelaide Cove PD earlier today. They'll probably receive it by lunch tomorrow."

My eyes dart around the room, bouncing between each of the men looming over me and the dozens of women pinned to the wall.

They're going to fucking get away with everything...

William fists the back of my shirt and lifts me from the chair forcibly. With the muzzle of the gun firmly pressed into my back, he shoves me through the house and out the front door.

"Move." William painfully jabs the barrel into me when I stutter as the gravel driveway digs into the soles of my bare feet.

"No one will ever believe I killed myself when I have muzzle bruises all over my back," I sneer. My vision quickly blackens at the edges when the butt of the gun cracks against my skull.

"No one is ever going to find your body," Edmund threatens as the four of them lead me to the trees lining my property.

"What is it that you said," Edmund steps before me when we reach them, "to Harper as I listened to you beat her within an inch of her life?"

He drops a duffel bag at his feet and unzips it before bending down and rifling through it. He pulls out two bundles of rope and hands them to Grant as he continues to dig in the bag.

"Oh, yes," he sighs as he slides a whip from it. "I thought you liked it rough."

CHAPTER
FORTY-THREE

EDMUND

Samuel holds Michales in a painfully tight grip as Grant skillfully ties knots around each of his wrists. Grabbing the slack hanging from his left hand, Grant secures the rope around a thick branch of one of the trees. With the other, he repeats the process, leaving Michaels strung between two trees with his arms in a deep V above his head.

Once Michales is held in place by Grant's meticulous knots, Samuel releases him. He struggles for a moment before releasing that it's futile.

Walking before him, whip in hand, I lean close before menacingly whispering, "You should know, I fucking love to make it hurt."

I stalk behind him and crack the whip to get a feel for it in my hand. *It's been a while.* By the time I turn around, Will and Samuel have spread a large tarp beneath his feet.

No evidence we were ever here.

"I enjoy inflicting in pain. Wicked, brutal pain, delivered in ways that I'd never expose Harper to." I crack the bullwhip, allowing just the tip to nip at his skin. Blood prickles through his white undershirt from the little bite popping open his flesh, and he cries out in pain. "But you...I'm more than fucking willing to show."

Quickly raising my arm, I crack the whip again. Michales howls as I let the thick thong of the leather slice down his back. It splits his shirt and the skin beneath, blood immediately trickling down his spine.

"You almost took her from me." I swing the whip again. He's still crying out when I crack it once more. "Every hand you laid on her is going to be repaid with your flesh and blood."

The whip cracks, echoing through the night like thunder. A vicious storm. Snapping the whip again and again, the flesh peels from his back with every flick of the handle and his pained howls become exhausted yelps.

When I finally stop, the muscles of my arm burn. My chest heaves from exertion, and sweat dampens my hairline. I swipe the back of my hand across my forehead to prevent it from dripping into my eyes.

Michales is slumped before me. The ropes digging through the flesh of his wrists as they force him to stay upright. Closing the distance between us, I note that some of the gashes along his back are so deep that I catch glimpses of bone through his shredded flesh and muscle.

His breaths are labored, and he teeters on the brink of unconsciousness.

We can't have that.

Samuel grabs a container of salt from the bag and sprinkles it generously over what is left of Michales's mangled back. He wails into the night, the burning pain forcing him to remain awake.

"No one...will...ever believe...I...k...killed myself," he stammers through labored breaths. "with...out...a...b...body."

"But they will." I slap his cheek to keep his attention on me when it begins to falter. "Because you told them. Right down to the coordinates where you anchored the fishing boat that you rented this afternoon."

He opens his mouth, but not a sound comes out. Once again, we are so many steps ahead of him that he never saw it coming.

Grant hacked into his finances this afternoon and used his credit card to secure the rental. William, adorning a pillow beneath his shirt to match Michales' build, took the boat from the harbor and left it anchored several miles offshore. Exactly in the location noted in confession where he described how he would end his misery and guilt.

When authorities find the boat empty, they'll assume he purposely went overboard. Ending his own life as cruelly as he ended the lives of all the women pinned to his office wall like trophies.

"Be happy that time is on your side," I cock as brow as Will steps behind Michales, "because I'd happily go at this for days. Stopping only when there wasn't a scrap of flesh left on your bones."

I tip my head, and Will snaps his neck. His legs immediately crumple beneath him, and he hangs from the ropes binding him to the trees.

"I'll get the SUV." Will wipes his bloodied hands across the front of his shirt. As he walks away, Grant and Samuel help me cut the ropes, causing Michales to drop onto the blood-covered tarp spread across the ground. Tossing the ropes and my whip onto his body, we securely roll every bit of evidence into the 12'x12' square of plastic.

The four of us load him into the plastic-lined trunk of the SUV and climb into our respective seats.

"Which street?" Will asks, expecting to be placing him with the other bodies we've left in this town.

"Not The Preserves." I shake my head. "Twilight Bluff."

The three of them turn to look at me, expecting an explanation. One I have no problem giving.

"The foundation of my new home is being poured in a few hours," I share. This build has been in the works for nearly a year. It was going to be an exciting place for me to play.

Instead, it's going to be my home...

...with Harper.

CHAPTER
FORTY-FOUR

EDMUND

With Harper's hand back in mine, I've been resting my head on the mattress beside her as I try unsuccessfully to garner a few hours of sleep.

Her fingers twitch in mine, and my head snaps to find her eyelids fluttering. Squeezing her hand, I breathe, "Little rose."

"Eh...Eddie." Her voice is raspy and pained.

"It's me." I pull her hand to my face and place a chaste kiss against her knuckles. "I'm here. I'm not going anywhere."

"Michales?" His name trembles from her lips.

"You don't need to worry about him." I run my fingers along her jaw, swiping away a rogue tear with the pad of my thumb. "He'll never lay a hand on you again."

Tears well in her eyes, and her voice cracks when she asks, "They caught him?"

"He'll never lay a hand on you again," I repeat .

"Eddie..."

"There are things you don't know about me, little rose,." I squeeze her hand a little tighter, expecting her to recoil from me. "Things you won't like."

"Did you kill him?" she poses her question in a faint whisper.

"Yes," I answer, short and truthfully.

And I'd end his life a thousand more times if I could.

Harper sucks in a sob, and tears begin to trickle silently down her cheeks. Climbing onto the bed, being careful not to hurt her, I cup her face and kiss away the tears. As my lips dust over her face, I confess, "I had to. He almost took you away from me. I couldn't let him——"

"I'm not crying because you killed him," she asserts as she interrupts me. "I'm happy he's fucking dead."

"There's more." I bury my face into the crook of her neck and tenderly kiss her. "So much more you don't know."

"Are you ever going to hurt me?" She presses her hand to my jaw, drawing my eyes up to hers.

"No, little rose," I answer. She would be the first in decades. The first since I learned what I was capable of or how easily I could cover my tracks. Yet, I am nearly certain in my answer.

I could never hurt her.

But I will happily hurt for her.

"Is it over?" she inquires. "Whatever happened in your life before me, is it over?"

"Yes." I nod, never breaking eye contact with her. "It's over."

Is Michales going to be the last man I kill?

Probably not.

A day will come when someone will stand in the way of something I want or have the audacity to put Harper in harm's way, and I will deal with it the only way I know how.

Swiftly.

Painfully.

Lethally.

But the string of disposable women buried throughout town—they are over.

The letter sent supposedly written by Detective Asshole made its way to the Adelaide Police Department a few hours ago. The entire department has been abuzz since. According to Will's inside guy, they are scrambling to ensure their asses are covered before this makes its way to the press within the hour.

Once that happens, all of us are in the clear of nearly every wrongdoing we've committed in this town.

"Then it doesn't matter, Eddie," she groans as she stretches forward to place a kiss against my lips. "It doesn't matter because I love you."

She lays back into her pillow, and while I know I should be gentle with her, my lips crash against hers. Slipping my tongue into her mouth, I kiss her deeply. Claiming her breaths and whimpers, inhaling her, and knowing I'll never get enough of her.

She's fucking ruined me.

Pulling back, my lips linger against hers, and I relish in the feel of her soft, warm breaths blowing against them.

"I love you, little rose." My lips vibrate against hers when I whisper, "And I will never be fucking done with you."

CHAPTER FORTY-FIVE

HARPER

About a week later...

Eddie has been arguing with the hospital staff—*and me*—for the last few days to let him take me home. As uncomfortable as this bed can be, and with how little there is to keep me occupied in this hospital room, I want to be well enough to know that I *can* take care of myself.

I am more than happy to have him dote on me, but I don't want him helping me on and off the toilet. It doesn't matter how willing to do so he is.

A girl needs some boundaries.

A little mystique.

We've been together a few months, not a few years. Convalescent care can wait a few decades.

While I'm still moving pretty slowly as I recover from my ruptured spleen, I'm finally mobile enough to concede to Eddie's barrage of requests to let him take me home.

Home...

"I'm surprised you lasted this long," the sweet, older nurse wheeling me downstairs teases. "That boy is a stubborn one."

"He is." I press my hand to my side as she causes me to chuckle. "Real fucking stubborn."

Eddie brings the car around and helps me into it as the nurse pushes the wheelchair back inside. Pulling out of the parking lot, he comfortingly places his hand on my thigh as he drives. He gives it a squeeze and asks, "Are you up for a quick stop on our way home? There's something I want to show you."

Instead of answering him, I look down at my current attire. A pair of Eddie's sweatpants that are big enough to hold two of me and his T-shirt that hangs almost to my knees. I haven't bothered with makeup in days. And while my hair is in a bun, it also hasn't seen a hairbrush since yesterday when Abigail graciously helped me with it.

"Just us." He squeezes my thigh again. "But I'd totally fuck you in that outfit."

"You haven't fucked me in a week. At this point, I'm surprised you can still walk with how swollen your balls must be," I jest.

"Is it that noticeable?" he quips as he turns onto a dirt road.

"Where are we going?" I ask as he drives slowly down the path while trying to avoid the large divots that will jostle me.

"*This* is what I wanted to show you."

"Is there even anything out here?" I inquire seconds before we reach the clearing. He pulls to a stop beside a construction site, but it's not what garners my attention. My eyes are locked on the view as Eddie walks around the car to help me from the low seat of his sports car.

It's fucking gorgeous.

"This is...just...wow," I exclaim to Eddie. We're parked on the bluff, overlooking the ocean and cove below. It's calming and serene. Absolutely perfect.

"You like it?"

"Who wouldn't?" I exhale. "It has to be absolutely breathtaking at sunrise."

"In three months, you can find out." He slips a key into my hand. "It's too late to change the framing, but otherwise, you can do anything you want."

"I don't understand." I shake my head, confused as to why he's giving me a house.

"I told you. I'm never going to be done with you." He palms my cheeks and places a soft kiss on my lips. "This is for us. A home that can be ours."

"Ours?" My lip quivers.

"*Ours.*"

"And I can do anything I want?"

"Almost." He pulls me gingerly into him. "The bedroom needs to look over the bluff. Because I can't stop thinking about you pressed against the glass, watching the sunrise as I slide into your ass."

I was quite certain an 'I love you' and building a home together in the same week was going to officially tap him out on romance, and it's comforting to know that I was right.

"You were wrong, you know." I wrap my arms around his waist.

"About what?"

"You." I press my face to his chest as I stare over the bluff. "There is more than a little good in you."

Eddie slips his finger under my chin and tips my face up to his, "Because of you. And *only* for you, little rose."

CHAPTER
FORTY-SIX

EDMUND

This entire fucking town has been a media circus. The only reason I am downtown and struggling through the current crowd at Latte Da is because Harper wants a crème brûlée latte.

And I'm a fucking simp for her.

A fucking simp dying to tie her to my bed and cover her healed body with new bruises.

My bruises.

My teeth.

My marks.

With the girls before her, I wouldn't have cared whether they were ready or not, but I can't fathom the idea of permanently hurting her.

A little pain on the other hand...

I mutter under my breath as my cock twitches

ts.

to think of anything other than Harper splay

my bed or sliding over my cock, I push my way i

fee shop. It is wall to wall with press. Not only

ıys, but the national chains.

escended upon Adelaide Cover seemingly overnig

ıem wanting to be the ones to get the big scoop

es. Yet, all of them regurgitate the same story.

there is no other story to be told.

the local paper from the counter, I read over

age.

Cobe News

Volume 10, Issue 5 2024

SERIAL KILLER COP

DETECTIVE DAVID MICHALES CONFESSES

Where Are They?

Confessing to all their deaths in his suicide note, David Michales refused to disclose the locations of any of his victims. Requested to remain unnamed, police sources have gone on record stating, "[Michales] suicide note referenced not wanting to disturb their final resting places as they deserve to finally have some peace."

While the girls all rest in peace, their families do not. Dozens of

Cop Killer

David Michales, former police officer of the Adelaide Cove Police Department has confessed to the brutal

Coast Guard has sworn off the search for his body, and at this time are speculating that the current has taken him outside

Local papers, tabloids, and national news coverage. Every last one of them pushing our agenda that Michales was responsible for every body we have buried beneath The Preserves.

Bodies no one will know exist until well after all of us are gone.

He might have been a more deplorable human being than any of the rest of us, but I have to give him credit for one thing.

He was a good fucking cop.

Unlike the rest of the police in this town, he saw us—*all of us devils*—for exactly what we are. He was missing one piece that would have taken us all down.

It's ultimately what led to him being condemned to an eternity below my future home. After what he did to Harper, I would have put him there with or without the help of Grant, Samuel, and Will. Their eagerness to help grew exponentially when they learned how close he was to exposing us.

I'm not naïve enough to believe their intentions were pure, and that they did it for me. I know this with certainty because none of us are built like that. Self-preservation above all else.

Only now, I'm not just protecting myself. I value Harper's life as much as my own.

Same as Samuel with Cora.

And I'm pretty sure with Grant and Abigail as well.

Refolding the paper, I set it back onto the counter and order Harper's drink. With the packed crowd, it takes a little longer than usual, but I'm back in the car and on my way home within minutes.

"Harper," I call as I walk through the door. When she doesn't answer, I begin wandering through the house looking for her. A splash comes from outside, and I am surprised to find her in the pool. A little angry, even, as I set her latte on the patio table. "What are you doing?"

Her doctors have been adamant about rest and relaxation as she recuperates. Exercise—or anything strenuous—has been off-limits since I brought her home.

"All my tests looked good yesterday." she smirks. "Doctor Vaughler said I could resume my normal activities, just that I needed to ease back into them."

I can ease her back in.

CHAPTER FORTY-SEVEN

HARPER

Hearing that my pussy is no longer off limits, I can't quite tell if Eddie is eager to fuck me or angry that I didn't tell him sooner.

Even if I did just find out ten minutes ago.

Reaching to his waist, his fingers work swiftly to undo the buckle of his belt.

Eager...

Definitely eager.

He kicks off his shoes as he pulls his shirt over his head.

Fuck he looks good.

Pushing his pants and boxers down his thighs, he kicks them from his feet before diving into the pool. He swims the length to me completely underwater. When he reaches me, he undoes the strings of my bikini bottoms. As they sink to the depths of the pool, his tongue licks along my pussy before he surfaces. The single touch tingles through my body like electricity.

The Eddie who has doted on me and treated me like a princess for the past couple of weeks has been great.

And exactly what I needed.

But there are no words to describe how I have missed the sadistic man who gets off on marking my body. The one who knows how to swing a paddle so hard it burns while setting my entire fucking body on fire.

That's the Eddie I need now.

Breaking the surface, tiny droplets splatter over my face as he slides his fingers through his sopping wet hair to push it away from his face. Beads of water continue to trickle down his face as reaches down to grab my thighs. As he lifts me up to him, I eagerly wrap my legs around his waist.

"I've missed the feel of my hands marking your skin," he growls against my neck as he roughly palms my ass. He squeezes hard—*blissfully hard*—causing me to wince at his short nails dimpling my skin. They dig deeper, slowly pressing through my flesh as he kisses and bites my shoulder.

His cock twitches between me, teasing and tapping at my entrance, and I move my hips, trying to take him inside me.

Needing him inside me.

"Have you missed my cock, little rose?" he gruffly chuckles against my neck as he tightens his grip on my ass to keep me from moving.

"Yes." I fight against his hold.

"As much as you've missed my sting on your skin?" He continues to hold me flush against him, sucking hard at just beneath my ear.

"More," I breathlessly moan.

Lifting me slightly, he impales me on his cock as he groans, "Not nearly as much as I've missed being inside you."

He buries the entirety of himself in me. Biting my lip to stifle the pain of being forcefully stretched to accommodate him, I let out a mewl of pure pleasure as he fills me.

Using the buoyancy of the water, he slides me over his length with ease. As he picks up his pace, the rippling water around us begins to splash against our bodies.

The needy ache from my pussy flutters in my stomach, and he continues to slide into me, building toward a release I've been yearning for weeks.

"You feel so fucking good wrapped around me." Eddie's arms envelop my waist as he pulls me tighter to him. Wanting—*and needing*—more, I squeeze my arms around his neck and my thighs around his waist, driving his thrusts even deeper.

Leaving one arm around me, he fists my hair and pulls my face onto his. He presses his lips to mine, but it's not enough for me.

I want his tongue in my mouth, aggressively exploring it as though he hasn't been there a thousand times before. Taking it roughly and claiming it as his.

Again.

Forever.

Abruptly closing the hair of distance between us, his mouth crashes against mine. The tongue I've been yearning for sweeps between my lips and plunges into my mouth. With both of us breathless, he pulls back and speaks through our kiss, "Come for me, little rose."

He buries himself in me, and I grind onto his hips, teetering on the edge of ecstasy as his lips and teeth tortuously travel the length of my neck. Reaching my ear, his voice is deep and commanding when he whispers, "I told you to fucking come for me."

As though his words have some magical power over me, I lose every bit of control when he begins to suck the already-bruised spot below my ear. My body explodes with electric waves of pleasure, and I cry out his name, clinging desperately to his body. I embrace him tighter and grind over him as I ride out my release. Trying desperately to prolong this feeling.

"One more," he demands seconds before gripping my ass and vigorously working my pussy over his length.

My sensitive clit rubs against the base of his hips with every savage thrust. Neither allowing me to fully recover from the first orgasm as the second begins to swell. It slams through me like the first, only this time, Eddie is thrust over the edge with me.

Groaning into each other's mouths, my pussy clenches as he spasms. Holding me tight and staying fully seated inside me, he pulls back from our kiss and growls, "Mine."

CHAPTER
FORTY-EIGHT

EDMUND

It's been a little over three months since Michales' death. The candlelight vigils for the women beneath The Preserves have ended. News vans and the press have slowly dwindled out of town.

Excluding the few wild as fuck conspiracy theories Grant found online, there hasn't been any suspicion regarding the validity of the narrative we told about his death. While we all knew he was determined to find us guilty for the things we had done, none of us knew how deep it had gone.

Those who worked with him and knew him well had been watching him fall apart for years. His ex-wife. His kids. Every member of the Adelaide Cove Police Department. The locals who have known him their entire lives.

They watched his obsession with us become all-consuming. A compulsion, eating away at every shred of the life he once had. The life he had before the five of us moved to town. The five of us granted excitement to his otherwise mundane and unremarkable existence.

His complete detachment from society, coupled with his incessant need to prove to everyone the wrongs we were committing, simply made believing that he was the devil in disguise that much easier for everyone.

His death was our new beginning, giving all of us a new life without *many* of our prior indiscretions hanging over our heads.

And bizarrely, Grant, Samuel, and I diving into some semblance of domestication.

Driving up to Twilight Bluff, I am not remotely surprised to pull in behind Harper's white Maserati Ghibli. She's practically lived here during daylight hours, overseeing every bit of the build. Meticulously managing every single detail to ensure that everything is absolutely perfect.

As with most times I've found her here, her arms are full of flooring, paint, and fixture samples, trying to finalize her plans. There's enough noise with the ongoing construction that I am able to sneak behind her with ease. Snaking my arms around her waist, I pull her back to me. She startles slightly before I manage to fully plant my kiss the crook of her neck.

"You're jumpy, little rose," I whisper against her ear while refusing to let her go. "Do you have a lot of men stealing an embrace when I'm not around?"

"I wasn't going to say anything, but Big Jim over there can be quite handsy at times."

I whip my head around to see who she's talking about, and she grips my face and turns it back to her.

"*I'm kidding.* The way you look at anyone who lets their eyes linger on me a tad too long, I can't fathom there is a man in this town that would have the balls to actually lay a hand on me."

She isn't wrong. She's mine.

While I do enjoy showing her off—*because she is fucking gorgeous*—I detest when men have the gall to think they have a chance with her.

With any man who tried, I would have no problem putting him six feet under. I'd dig up the foundation with my bare hands and lay him beside Michales. A collection of men who had the audacity to think they deserved to know what my little rose feels like.

A sly smile tugs at my lips from the thought. I may have been granted the opportunity to start a new life, but it doesn't mean I've become a fucking saint.

"Come on." I slip my fingers into hers. "It's time to go home."

"Five more minutes." She squeezes my hand and fights against my pull.

"No." My voice is deep and authoritative.

"Eddie?" she coos playfully.

Stepping to where she stands steadfast, I slip my hand around her throat and place a rough kiss against her lips. Lingering close and keeping my voice low, I whisper, "I said it's time to go. If I have to throw you over my shoulder and drag you home to play with my sweet little cunt, you're going to be very sorry."

"Fine," she huffs. "Just let me grab my ba—"

Her words are cut short with a squeal as I grab her waist, hoist her over my shoulder, and carry her back to my car. Not caring who sees, I turn my head and sink my teeth into the perfectly round ass cheek before me.

I expect her to yelp from the force, but instead, I'm met with a lusty groan. Taking a deep breath, I manage to maintain a steady gate as I make my way to my Bacalar.

I don't put her down or open her door. I pull her into the driver's seat with me and shut the door.

She's going to regret not listening the entire way home.

CHAPTER
FORTY-NINE

HARPER

Parked no more than one hundred feet from the construction site that's swarming with workers, Eddie tears at the button of my shorts. I struggle against him, but his muscular arm around my waist has me practically pinned to him.

When he gets them below my knees, he pushes the ignition and peels away from the site. He roughly shoves his fingers into my pussy and growls, "Don't ever deny me of my fucking cunt."

With one hand on the steering wheel and the other aggressively working my pussy, I writhe on his lap as he quickly works me to the edge.

"Fuck, Eddie," I groan as my back arches, and I grind down on his hand. He thrusts deep and massages his fingers against my walls, rubbing over the spot inside that does me in. Panting, I fist his shirt and grip his thigh.

I'm so fucking close.

Eddie stills his fingers and takes his time sliding them from me, ripping away the orgasm that was only seconds away. Lifting his arousal-covered fingers from between my thighs, he shoves them into my mouth and snarls, "You want to keep me from my cunt? I'll keep you from coming."

He drives down the winding roads with his fingers in my mouth long after I've sucked them clean. Pulling them from my mouth, he plunges them back between thighs. He teasingly rubs his fingers around my clit, occasionally thrusting inside me—but not once letting me come.

He toys with me the entire drive home, leaving me so fucking needy that I could scream. As he pulls to a stop before the front steps of our current home, he opens the door and slides me from his lap. My shorts fall around my ankles as he helps me to my feet.

He climbs from the car and looms over me with dark eyes. "If you want to come tonight, I expect you naked and bent over our bed by the time I get there."

I don't run inside, but I take a brisk pace, ensuring that I beat Eddie. I've played this game with him before, and while he makes up for it in the morning, he is not above letting me go to sleep left wanting.

Stripped bare, I have my feet firmly planted on the floor and my chest pressed to the mattress when Eddie walks through the door holding two paddles.

Walking behind me, he immediately rubs the smooth leather along my ass and thighs. A tingle runs down my spine as he warms my skin, my heart beginning to race as I remember what the paddle feels like when it strikes my skin.

When he pulls back, I know the sting I crave is coming. Until he denies me of that, too.

"I hope you're ready, little rose, because I intend to take my time with you."

I'm about to speak when the paddle thuds against my ass, causing me to whimper in delight.

"Is that what my little pain slut wants?" He rubs the paddle over my stinging skin as he slips three fingers inside me, "Or does she want to come?"

His fingers work me so fervently as his thumb rubs over my clit that I can't bring myself to muster a single word. On the cusp of coming, he quickly withdraws them and provides my ass with several swats of the paddle.

"Look at you," he croons. "Fucking dripping for me." He licks his tongue up my inner thigh, groaning as he laps up the arousal spreading across my thighs. He keeps licking until he reaches my pussy. Kneeling behind me, his tongue swirls around my sensitive clit, licking and sucking as though he cannot get enough of me.

"Fuck you taste good." His muffled words vibrate against my pussy, causing my thighs to tremble. "So fucking good I almost can't stop."

"Don't..." I pant as I push back toward his retreating tongue.

"Almost ready for me." He rubs his warm palm over my ass. His hand is quickly replaced with the paddle, the cool leather dusting over my warm skin. He strikes again, and the thud burns my ass. Another, and then he moves to the other cheek.

My ass on fire and my pussy aching with need, Eddie bends himself over my body. Using my hair for leverage, he turns my neck toward him and kisses my lips.

"Five more." He holds a new paddle before me. The second I see it, I gulp, and my heart begins to race.

"I...I can't," I stammer, seeing the thin metal tines protruding from the wood. Shaking my head, I panic at the thought.

"You can take it." His deep voice vibrates straight to my pussy. "You'll take it like the perfect little pain slut you are, and you'll fucking love each one."

Climbing from the bed, he takes his place behind me. His hand rubs over my back and softly says, "Grip the sheets, breathe, and enjoy how fucking good it hurts."

He gently swings the paddle, and it hits with a thousand bites. A broken, breathy scream rattles from my lungs as my toes curl.

It hurts so fucking good.

CHAPTER
FIFTY

EDDIE

Swinging back again, I gently come down on her other cheek. Leaving them both covered in pricks from the paddle. Tiny droplets of blood pooling from the tines.

She yelps when I land the third strike of the paddle. Her legs tremble as she awaits the fourth, but I can hardly pull my eyes from her quivering cunt. Or the arousal practically cascading down her thighs.

"You're doing so fucking good for me." I rub my hand over her hip. "Two more for me, little rose."

Staring back at me, her lower lip quivers, and tears well in her eyes as she nods .

She cries through the final two swats of the paddle. They leave her ass a stunning shade of crimson, a thin smear of blood covering over the marks I've left on her.

"You look so fucking gorgeous for me." I fist the shaft of my cock and align it to her entrance. "Taking my pain until you bleed."

Pressing my cock inside of her, I slowly bury myself to the hilt. The blood on her ass and arousal coating her thighs smears across my body, I bend over her and kiss up her spine.

"You did so fucking good for me." I kiss a tear from her cheek while slowly rocking my hips. She presses her tender ass into me, silently begging for more.

I take my time, fucking her deep and slow as I run my fingers along her body.

There isn't an inch of her I don't want to mark.

Not an inch I don't want to savor.

Her cunt quivers around my cock, and I need her come nearly as much as she does. Picking up my tempo, I kiss along the backs of her shoulders and whisper, "Are you going to come for me?"

"Yes." She lets out a pained whimper.

"Show me," I thrust hard and deep. "Show me how you fucking come for me."

I take her faster, keeping the brutal thrusts until she moans into the sheets beneath her and writhing her hips against me.

"I'm never going to fucking get enough of you," I groan as she comes, and her slick cunt convulses around me.

I begin to fuck her at a punishing pace for us both. One I know I will do me in, but I need more from her. I want her a quivering, bloody mess beneath me.

Gripping her hips, I fuck her into the mattress with such force it inches across the bed. Her cries of pleasure fill the room as she loses herself for me over and over again. Sweat glistens down her spine as she orgasms to exhaustion.

My own sweat beads my hairline and trickles down my chest as I relentlessly fuck her. Still wanting more of her, I can't hold back. My balls tighten, and my cock grows more rigid inside of her. I'm fucking done for. Slamming to her, her entire body trembles as my cock twitches inside of her. Her hips grind against me through every spasm as I fill her with my cum and mark her as mine.

Buried deep inside of her, I rub my fingers along her sweaty skin as we both try to slow our deep, heavy breaths. Pulling my cock from her, I scoop her exhausted body into my arms and place her on the bed. I pull open the drawer of the nightstand and grab a cleansing towelette to thoroughly clean the dried blood from her backside.

"Could you be any more perfect for me?" I pose the rhetorical question as I climb into the bed beside, pull her close and wrap my body around her.

"Or you for me," she sleepily mutters as she nestles herself into my chest.

EPILOGUE

EDMUND

Harper stirring slightly in her sleep wakes me. Her hair is splayed over my arm, and her face is nestled against my pec. Staring down at her, I'm still in awe that after three years of waking up beside her, I'm as infatuated with my wife as I was the first night I met her.

Gorgeous.

Intelligent.

Witty.

And an insatiable appetite for both my pain and my cock.

Slipping out from beneath her, I make my way under the sheets and gently part her thighs. She's spread wide with her cunt on display for me, and I lightly slide my tongue from her entrance to clit. A feather light touch that causes a breathy moan to pass over her lips without fully waking her. I continue to teasingly lick and lightly suck at her, savoring her as I take my time increasing my touch and rousing her from her slumber.

"Fuck, Eddie," she groans sleepily as her fingers slide into my hair. "You can't keep waking me like this."

"Good morning, beautiful. I will wake you however I see fit." My words vibrate against her cunt as I say them between kisses. The flat of my tongue firmly swirling against her clit, I slip my middle finger into her ever-ready cunt with ease. Working my tongue and finger in tandem, Harper is quickly breathless and panting. She lets out a sad, disappointed groan when I pull my finger from her.

"Don't worry, little rose. You're going to come all over my fingers and tongue." I let my spit and her arousal dribble from my lips to the tight, puckered hole between her cheeks. Using my arousal-covered finger, I massage my saliva around her hole and press into her. Easing into her and stretching out her tight hole, I slide another finger into her cunt. I thrust into both of her holes and slather her inner thigh with wet kisses, "And then you're going to take my cock as I punish your gorgeous fucking ass."

I drive my fingers into her, filling both of her holes, as I fervently lick and suck at her clit. Her fingers tangle in my hair, gripping it and roughly dragging my tongue to exactly where she wants me. Holding me there, she grinds against my face as I curl my fingers inside her. The breaths and whimpers trembling over her lips become more rapid and broken. Her hips quickly shake as her thighs begin to quiver against my face. I drag my teeth over her clit, and it throws her over the edge. Her body spasms, and she painfully tugs at her fistful of my hair, moans rattling from her as she comes undone beneath me.

Not giving her the opportunity to recover from her euphoric high, I roll her onto her stomach and press the throbbing head of my cock against her welcoming ass. Gripping her hips, I stretch her wide as I ease my cock into her ass, groaning, "I plan to spend my day filling each of your holes. Fucking you full of cum, until it fucking drips from you as a reminder of who you belong to."

Wrapping her hair around my fist, I pull back hard, forcing a stunning curve of her back while putting her ass further into the air. I take my time fucking her tight hole, using my free hand to thoroughly tan her ass a gorgeous shade of scarlet as she repeatedly comes around my cock.

My perfect little pain slut.

Pleased with my work, with my balls aching for release, I pick up my pace. My hips slam against her ass, and the sounds of our skin clapping together echoes around the room like an ovation. I drive into her one final time with a roar, burying in to the hilt as I unload my seed into her.

Kneeling behind her with my cock still buried in her ass, I release my firm hold on her hair and run my fingers along her spine. Leisurely enjoying her a little while longer as we watch the sun peek over the horizon.

"It's so fucking beautiful," Harper exhales while she stares out the window overlooking the bluff.

My eyes roam over the handprints on her ass as I share her view out of our bedroom window. Amazed at the life I've built with her, I whisper to myself, "It sure fucking is."